HALF A
MILE FROM
TUCSON

A DEAD
WESTERN

BRIAN
NANN

For all those searching for the sound

1: LORDSBURG

Clouds gathered atop the Peloncillo and sat churning over the raw peaks. Holding there for hours, the clouds swept down the east face of the range and unleashed a wind across the playa. Sweeping billows of sand tumbled out of the blackness and dwarfed the jagged lines along the terrible horizon. Shimmering lights swung from their posts, marking refuge for those seeking shelter from the harsh conditions of the idle boxcars along the Southern Pacific. Every two-bit hotel and stable claimed no vacancy on this evening, on account of the evacuation of sleeper cars, filled with northern tourists. As well, count the miners in from the brown folded mountains surrounding this outpost of saloons and supply stores that arose with the blessing of the company.

The grainy blackness of the high desert wilderness matched the hidden corners and back rooms of Wheat's Saloon. Light sputtered from dim stubby candles scattered across tables and lined against the back door, leading toward the jakes. Lamps burned low behind the bar where James

Wheat, a slim man in a starched white shirt, rubbed the inside of a glass with a starched white towel. Two miners sat next to each other on a bench, their elbows resting on the tabletop. They hunched over and stared into their whiskey like sooth-sayers peering into a vile caldron for some future truth, distant but ill-fated. The miner took his hat off and dropped it on the floor. He moaned or he spoke, the barman could not tell and beyond that moment, did not wonder.

A steady rap on the door echoed through the empty saloon and the pulse of the thump began to rattle the hinges. The miner with the red bandana around his eye stared at the door and said, "Is some poor fool failing to make his appearance or the storm fixing to carry us off?"

James Wheat looked over at the entrance and said, "It's bound to pick up."

And whether he was making reference to the clientele or the wind the miners did not know. But the door did bolt open and the errant winds howled through the open portal between the two hellish worlds. Into that saloon the storm brought a group of dust-covered men, who began to pat themselves down with a loud fury and caused the sand to burst from their clothes in vanishing clouds cascading to the floor.

The men shuffled toward an empty wooden table in the far corner of the room. Creaking of bones and cries of exhaustion filled the saloon as the benches bent under the weight of the travelers. James Wheat continued rubbing his glass and held it up to the faint light above the bar.

2

"What'll it be?"

A voice came from the table, "Four beers. One whiskey."

"Four beers. One whiskey."

James Wheat placed the clean glass under the tap and began to pour the silt-hued beer. He grabbed the next glass with his free hand and raised the glass to the light in his search for spots. After filling the order he walked the libations around the bar to their table. The men nodded and drank in silence, the only sound being the subdued howl and shriek of that storm battering down upon the saloon. James Wheat spat in a glass, grabbed the towel and with two fingers rubbed the inside. The miner, with hat now back on his head, straightened himself and said, "I hear in eighty-nine the damn storm ripped up the track twenty mile."

A voice from the table spoke up. "Barkeep? You hear that?"

James Wheat looked toward the far corner and lifted his eyebrow. "Sandstorm like this in eighty-nine? Believe it was eighty-eight. Indeed. Eighty-eight. Steins impassible. Reckon that's so now. You all headed west?"

The figures at the table did not answer and the miners gazed again for their fortune. The miner removed his bandana. "I guess they is," he said.

A Mexican boy with dark, sunken eyes joined the proprietor as the storm swelled the pool of refugees in the saloon. He wore a white linen shirt stained with the yellow dust of the desert. He took a chair from the back door and pulled it across the floor next to the bar. There he awaited for smudged empty glasses to collect or penny cigars to pass out when called upon. When the door would open, another group of men, two or three, would find a place at the dark wooden bar or a seat at the crude tables. The din began to rise, growing to laughter. The howling of sand and low thuds of shutters slamming faded under the jabber and grunting of the patrons.

The bar hosted Fong who sat smoking a long pipe. Through the smoke he stared at the rugged sea of miners, brakemen, Mexicans and tramps. A man from the back emerged from the darkness and into the layer of fog that draped over the bar.

"Shannon, bring another beer," a voice ordered.

The man turned. "Aye," he said and gave a wave.

He was of medium height and his brown overcoat hung from his shoulders. The fedora had left a mark on his forehead and his straight hair hung just above his brow and bounced when we walked. His face was hardened by dirt and sun but his smile gave off a glow that most would say brought him youth. He looked down the bar and the Mexican boy caught his nod and approached.

"Two beers and a whiskey, lad."

The boy nodded and turned. Above the bar a tin American flag was pinned next to a shelf of empty green whiskey bottles. The bottles sparkled in the reflection of the mirror and cast over the flag a queer hue. The Mexican boy brought over the shot of whiskey. The man fingered the glass, rose it up and toasted.

"To Old Glory." Up came his hand as he threw back the shot and then slammed it back down onto the bar. The Mexican boy was still standing there. "My two beers, son. My two beers. Go on."

From behind the veil of smoke spoke Fong. "You in on the road?"

"In from road?"

Fong nodded as if to ask the question again or to agree with the man's interpretation of it. The strands of smoke had hints of myrrh and it slithered from the side of his mouth as a boa slithers down a thick trunk.

"Aye, in from the road. Long stretch from Deming in this blow."

"I Fong," he said as another cloud spewed forth from the corner of his mouth.

"You Fong. I Shannon. Pleasure."

Fong said, "Shannon," and nodded again.

Shannon looked down the bar and the Mexican boy scampered toward him holding two lagers that bubbled and foamed, spilling over the rim and baptizing the boy's foot. Shannon paid the boy. He collected the coin and then disappeared under the bar. Shannon followed him with his gaze. The boy bent over a small mouse and stroked the creature's tail, feeding the animal a small crumb of bread. Fong saw this and nodded.

Fong said, "How you find Deming?"

"I'll find it in hell next time I'm there. Bastards. The lot. The damn whole town. One bastard in particular. Burned his name right here." Shannon took his finger and trapped the side of his head. "Right there, Mr. Fong. Right there. You can count on it. Bastard's name is McGlinchy." Fong nodded. "Do you know the son of a bitch? He pistol-whipped Connor. Barely made it back to the freight, we did. But, no worries, Mr. Fong. He'll get what is coming to him."

Fong nodded. "Same here."

"Same here what?"

"You find in Deming. You find here. Same here."

Shannon peered through the smoke. Fong nodded. For what reason Shannon did not know and it occurred to him he was indeed unsure of his past nods.

Fong said, "Your friend? Need medicine?"

"Whiskey suits his wears at the moment."

"You need medicine. See me. Down street. Last alley. Fong Laundry. You ask."

James Wheat let any man sleep where he lay for whatever the man could muster from his pocket. Those who refused or passed on the offer were wished a good evening and ushered out of the saloon with the door barred behind them. The

Mexican boy was seen leaving from the back door followed by Fong. The howling and creaking replaced the laughter and shouting once again as the lamp was extinguished. The heavy breathing and wheezing of the dirty denizen sang out like the squeals of bats in the pitch darkness.

The sun rose cold and cast soft shadows on the weathered and pitched lumber of the framed town. Brakemen and engineers stood in the easy morning light, their breath showing as they toiled to wake the slumbering iron horses under their charge. The citizenry began to step outside to survey the morning and any damage left from the storm. Children swept sand off the steps of the general store while Mother watched from the window above. Their heads jerked when a shotgun blast rang down Main Street. An old woman drew the curtain and pressed her cheek against the cold glass, her nostrils stamping a foggy impression across the windowpane. Two men stepped out of the barber shop and looked down the corridor.

The shot sounded like a wet thud inside the saloon. Shannon sat up, his hat tumbling off his head. James Wheat circled the bar, cutting across a beam of sun, littered with twirling dust. Connor rose with Shannon and the three men stepped out on the porch to find a skinny, disheveled man walking toward them with shotgun folded over his shoulder. James Wheat put his hand above his brow to better make this silhouette approaching. Shannon looked at Connor and they both looked at this figure drenched in a corona of sun.

James Wheat said, "Jesus, Jack. What's the trouble?"

"No trouble J.W."

The left pocket of his white shirt had been removed and in its place, a patch of solid black canvas. His hair fell to his shoulders and a faded scar ran from the left corner of his eye to ear. His beard now approached a month on and within it hid as many beads of sand. His overalls hung from a single strap and he appeared to have no other belongings on his person other than the shotgun now held over the back of his neck. One hand gripped the butt and the other, the barrel.

James Wheat said, "I barely recognized you without that damn hat of yours. Where it at?"

"Lost it in that damn wind last night."

"You were out in that?"

"Just some. Got caught coming back from the ranch."

"Well. What is all the damn shooting about then, Jack?"

"That? Came across this burro buried in about ten foot of sand, I reckon. Must have slid off the damn roof of the supply barn next to the stockade. Just lying there moaning. Damn tongue out its mouth. Dry as a bone the thing. I done it a favor."

"Suppose you did, Jack. Suppose you did."

Jack spat and offered his hand. "Howdy. Jack."

"Shannon. This here is Connor."

Jack snapped the shotgun back into form and tucked it under his arm. "Lovely town this time of year, ain't it?"

James Wheat stood with his hand on his hip and a rag dangling from his left hand. He hoisted the rag and waved the cloth with some alarm when a group of men rounded the general store on Main armed with rifles. They stopped upon the sight of the signal and a few of them waved and all turned back.

James Wheat said, "Folks are restless in this country. Let's head in before one of us gets shot." The men agreed and turned back into the saloon.

The shot had stirred the rest of the sleeping patrons. One stood dreary at the bar. It was the miner, who pulled his hat over his eyes and stared himself down in the mirror. Jack pulled alongside the miner and said, "Looks like ye might find this morning kinder with another drink, friend."

"I ain't your friend." The miner wheezed.

James Wheat said, "Now don't be that way, Walter."

Jack came around the side of Shannon and placed the shotgun on the bar. "J.W., can you secure this for me? And I will be sure to ignore the bastard. He just spent too much of his damn life in a hole. How many years now, Walt?"

"Eight years," Walt moaned. "I'm fixing to quit."

"Heard that one."

A draft came from the back door and with it brought the ash and smoke of a cook fire ignited to boil coffee. The Mexican boy stood over the deep pot and stirred. James Wheat took hold of the shotgun and ducked under the bar.

After rising, he produced a tin of tobacco from a box behind the till and opened it on the bar. He began to roll cigarettes. Shannon rolled one for Walt. Connor wrapped his tobacco and walked to the back door. He took a stick from the fire, lit his cigarette and put his hands to the warmth. The smoke split his face and blew through the bar and out the front door.

The Mexican boy poured grinds into the boil and began to stir with a wooden ladle. Connor watched him from across the fire. The crushed beans transformed the water and foam began to simmer on the surface. Connor held a tin vessel, ready to receive this sacrament of the newly shorn day. The boy looked up at Connor and said, "Café," and continued to stir. Connor looked at the boy and the boy said nothing further that morning.

Shannon drew his nose to the dark smell, dragged deep on his cigarette and said, "Sure does remind a man of home."

"What home is that?"

"Jack, that there is a loaded question."

"If ye don't care to say, damn sure don't have to."

"Tir Na Nog."

Jack looked at Shannon and blew a long line of smoke before him. James Wheat stepped out to sweep the porch. Jack reached over the bar and grabbed a bottle of unmarked whiskey.

"Drink?"

Shannon hung the cigarette from his lip. "A bit early?"

"I generally don't care for a man who can't answer a straight one."

"Pour, old boy. Pour."

"This is hostile country for tramps now. Best watch yourself if ye aim to extend the visit."

Shannon hoisted and drank his tumbler. With his thumb and forefinger he pinched the drop of whiskey off his bottom lip. Connor now had the steaming brew in a beat tin cup and he called in to the men to tally their preference. Shannon took a seat in front of the smoldering fire and rubbed his hands into the radiance of the warmth. The sun touched distant hills and cast an orange impression along the top of the makeshift fence lining the yard of the saloon, in its boundaries a pile of rail spikes and twenty foot of rusted chain. In the far corner sat a split anvil, which on top sat a raven that stared at the fire. Jack whistled at the bird and the thing squawked and flapped off over the roof.

Over coffee they rolled fresh cigarettes and Jack passed around a box of matches found behind the bar.

"Keep them," he told Shannon.

"Tell me, Jack. What of this burg and the hostile climate?"

"Nothing ye can really have done about it. The Southern Pacific wreck of the No. 20. Big news in these parts at least. Whole damn thing flew off the track after hitting a broken

11

rail. Lots of decent folks in them cars, don't you know? Even had doctors in from Tucson on account of all the injured. No deaths but I suppose only by the grace of the Lord."

Connor said, "And the rail?"

Shannon said, "Aye, the rail," as he poured a shot of whiskey into his coffee. He put the bottle down, made the cross and kissed his fingers.

Jack continued, "Damn rail. Ripped out. On purpose the Southern Pacific stiffs would have ye believe. Couldn't prove none different either. Well, wouldn't you know some damn gang of hoboes made a scene the week before. Said they was gonna rip up the tracks. They done made their conclusions. There you have it. They started rounding up your kind from El Paso to Tucson. Not pretty from what I hears. How did ya'll find Deming?"

"Let's not talk about Deming," said Connor.

Shannon stood and held his back. "Ah, well, Jack. They gave it to us."

"I am afraid ye liable to find the same here. Best lay low. The storm was a blessing for ye arrival. Likely the bulls would have aimed to take their piece of you. Along with Hughes."

Shannon said, "Who now is Hughes?"

"Hughes. Night watchman. Works the depots but won't show his face round this end. If you stay clear of the street you'll beat the vagrancy charge the deputy will bring on ye."

A pack of dogs circled the outside of the fence and the panting gave way to digging under the backside. James Wheat ran out and yelled, "Now git!" He threw a stick that smacked hard against the fence and sent the dogs scampering. "Grease on them coals brings them dogs out. Keep telling that boy to watch that damn grease. Where is he anyhow?"

James Wheat disappeared back into his dark saloon, where the clinking of glass and the low drag of chairs and tables could be heard. Connor made circles with his decrepit boot in the dirt, threw his cigarette in the middle and spat on it. Shannon thumbed his hat over his hairline and said, "So where could a man lay low in this burg?"

Jack spat. "Laying low. I don't have to think hard about that one. Where is that boy?"

Tall strands of yucca swayed in a wind left over from the storm, the stalks glowing against the backdrop of tanned hills. The back door to Fong's Laundry was made of a sturdy wood not seen in this country. Jack knocked on the door and Shannon ran his index finger over the smooth exterior admiring the work. The door opened. There stood the Mexican boy and behind him Fong, who gestured with both hands to enter. Shannon paused at the threshold. Connor peeked over his shoulder.

"Please, please," said Fong.

Connor studied the lay of the room before succumbing to Fong's invitation. He looked back at the boy as he barred the door behind them. Shannon took off his hat and placed it on a wooden peg. On the wall hung a scroll, the sides frayed from travel and age. The green landscape was clear though faded. Towering mountains loomed over a solo traveler, a red hat pulled tight over his head, a satchel strung across his back.

"You do same," said Fong. Connor took off his hat and found an empty peg on the wall.

Fong said, "Please." He gestured toward a dark hallway and led them to a door. Fong pulled a key and turned the knob in such a motion, one might suspect a magic trick. "Please. I knew you come. See you last night." Fong nodded. "You pick one." Jack had already taken his spot on a yellow mat, his head propped on the long, crusty pillow.

"Lay, lay," Fong said to Connor who stood stiff over his mat.

Connor slowly removed his coat. The Mexican boy hung it over a stubby hook protruding from the emerald wallpaper, a section of the interior peeling where there appeared to be water damage. Black rings dotted the area. Connor lay down and propped his head on a rank pillow, one that perhaps hosted the head of a thousand others. Across from where he lay, a wall scroll depicted a rat and hare in humanoid form, both adorned in Eastern robes and flanked by symbols. The men knew not what they read and did not ask. Fong bent down and kneeled in front of Connor. Their eyes met and Fong motioned to the

Mexican boy. He carried over a tray with the necessary accoutrements. Connor said, "What's that boy's name?"

"He no name. He no talk."

"He spoke to me."

"Did he say name?"

"No, he said café."

Fong touched Connor's shoulder and put the pipe to his lips. The glow off the lamp cast long shadows over Fong's face, his eye sockets like two bottomless holes. Fong said, "He say coffee. Coffee. Please?"

He pressed the bowl of the pipe toward the chimney of the lamp. The opium slowly vaporized. Connor stared down the end of the molded glass. The glow stretched further away. He grew cross-eyed and a glaze came over his sight like the veneer of rain on a window. Through that window, Connor saw the Mexican boy waving to him.

Connor said, "Coffee." A rattle in his throat became the word and he took another long inhale and watched the smoke slither between the rat and the hare and was then thankful for their guardianship over him in that moment. Fong rubbed the fold of hair that hung over his forehead. He turned and nodded toward the boy.

Jack said, "You ever partook before?"

"Aye, Beaumont on a failed trip back home. Long story, Jack."

Fong offered assistance to Shannon and he turned onto his right side and faced Jack.

Jack said, "Shannon, you speak in riddles. Anyone ever mention that to ye?"

Shannon rolled his head back over toward the ceiling. Shapes danced on the walls and formed arms stretching in all directions. Jack watched him. Shannon said, "I'm Irish, don't you know?"

"Never could have guessed."

Fong sat in the corner and rocked back and forth as he sang folk songs from childhood. He would pause and laugh in between verses, a soft laugh as if no one was there. The door would open and close. Open and close and then it did not.

"Jack! Jack! Git your ass up, boy."

Jack woke in a deep sweat, and a pong of wet grass and dirt filled the small room. The voice came through the curtains. The door swung open.

"Jack, git ur ass up. Ye outa the wagon today. Boss said it's your go to ride drag and he said he don't give a half damn if ye ain't feeling up to snuff yet." Jack said nothing and stared at the man. His sleeve wiped the sweat running off his temple. "Well," said the man. "Git your ass up then."

Jack rose and searched for his boots. He opened his mouth to speak but dust dropped from the roof of his mouth. He palmed the coarse wood and then grabbed both boots and put each on the wrong foot. A stream of light through the dark curtain sawed the aroma of perspiration in the room and from the crack in the curtain, he viewed a herd of shifting beasts. He could perceive snorting and calves calling for mothers and tugging at tough pink nipples. Jack could then realize the colors and the incessant chewing of that herd and yet nothing made a noise in that twirling chaos outside of the curtain. Jack put his palms on the floor and grains of dirt sifted through his fingers. He could not push himself up. He seized the curtain and he looked up to hear the rings beginning to pop and that made a noise and he could hear the call.

"Jack! Jack! Git ur ass up, boy!"

"Jack."

Shannon lay beside him. Jack sprung. "Where am I?"

Shannon said, "Fong's. Fong's Laundry."

Jack felt for his hat but could not find it.

"You looking for your hat? You lost your hat in the storm, Jack."

The room was empty save for two lamps and dancing shadows the silver sleeves cast upon the walls. Missing was the tray, along with Fong, the Mexican boy, and Connor. Shannon said, "Where on earth he wander off to?"

Next to him he found a small pitcher of water, which he gripped and pulled heartily from. He handed it over to Jack whose throat finished off the remains. Shannon stood and turned to face Jack with his hand stretched downward, and Jack grabbed his hand and with a boost was on his feet. The door was found ajar, albeit slightly and the hall revealed pitch darkness. The only light that beckoned was a lamp in the back room, where they had entered sometime before. Shannon grabbed his hat off the hook and shook it before placing it back on his head. Connor's hat was gone.

"Need to get me another hat," Jack said. "A man in this country needs a hat."

Shannon said, "You don't suppose the time?"

"I can't suppose a damn."

Shannon cracked the back door. The moon peeked through the crack and stood naked and bright in the sky over the inky hills to the north. Shannon said, "Night. Been out for a dog's age, we have."

Jack said, "Best get moving."

"And where to?"

"I know a place."

"I hope not a place we can lay low again?"

"How does cheap grub and a stiff drink sound?"

Shannon said, "I will save my reply till after both."

Jack motioned toward the dark hall and led Shannon down the corridor to the front room. A register sat on the counter, the floor strewn with stuffed white canvas bags tightly packed and tied. The moonlight cast a silver tone through the double windows where the etching across read Fong's Laundry. Jack grabbed the doorknob. Before turning, he reached above him and grabbed the bell to stop its double ring. Jack said, "The saloon ain't far. Just a few down but always a chance of running into the deputy. He'll be sure to stop me if he don't recognize ye. So keep your eyes down."

The street was still and had little traffic to speak of. Piano could be heard muffled in the distance and faded into the night as they walked toward their destination. Two cowboys passed on the opposite side of the road. One carried a chicken by its feet. The other cupped his hands and blew into them. After they passed, Shannon looked back and they were gone.

"Got to get me a damn hat."

"Even under that fur I suppose you call hair?"

"This fur here gotten me through, partner. Damn sure do not want to feel a night up in the Dragoons."

"Certainly doesn't sound pleasant."

"It ain't. Yonder." Jack raised his chin and bumped Shannon's left arm. "There she is. La Cabeza."

The facade wore a faded white tone with maroon shutters to match. The second story was battered, displaying a trail of weather and time. Horses stood tied in front of the saloon, one watered. The others huffed as the men passed and climbed the stairs. Shannon said, "And what do you suppose La Cabeza means?"

"The head, man. It means the head in Spanish. I ain't never inquired. Tonight will be none different."

The saloon expelled a gush of warm air as they entered. Their skin felt the touch of heat. Sparks flew up and twirled out of a fire a man stood poking. The bar was lively with a fiddler on the far playing a high melody. The men withdrew their coats and hung them on antlers that decorated the walls by the hundreds. Some horns hosted hats, others decorated with trinkets and scarves of patrons long gone. A pronghorn head adored the mirror above the bar, presiding over all who sat and wished to drink under its eternal glare.

Jack slapped the bar counter. "Here is fine."

"I've no money, Jack."

"Didn't suspect you did. Get me back when ye strike it rich."

Jack flagged down the barman, deep in conversation with a group of men by the fiddler. One of the men nodded and the barman turned and with his two hands tucked inside his apron yelled, "Jack Straw from Shakespeare!" The barman walked down behind the bar with his hands still inside his apron. "I indeed was beginning to worry about you. But looks like I have done worried enough 'bout ye. Here you are."

Jack said, "Here I am, Leroy. Worrying about me is like worrying about a dog and his bone. Don't make a lick of sense."

"Sure as hell don't, Jack. Who's your friend here?"

"This here is Shannon. Shannon, this here is Leroy Keith. Proprietor of the La Cabeza."

Shannon said, "A pleasure I'm sure."

"All mine. All mine indeed. So where you from, Shannon? Cannot seem to place that coming off your tongue."

"That place would be New Orleans, Mr. Keith."

"Oh dear. Long way from home aren't you? No worries, Shannon. Ran into a character all the way from New Jersey here last week. If you can believe that one? Hope Jack filled you in on the welcome wagon for men such as yourself in Lordsburg."

"Indeed. Jack gave me the particulars."

"Glad to hear it. And please, my friends call me Leroy."

"I will be sure to remember that."

Leroy Keith hooked his thumbs around his suspenders, ran them up, back down and then patted his stomach and said, "Can I get you gentlemen some supper?"

Shannon said, "Leroy, now you're speaking my language."

Leroy whistled as he walked down from behind the bar and swung out of sight. After a few minutes he appeared with two plates of machaca and tortillas for both men. The steam from the plates rose and enveloped Shannon's face. He took a deep inhale and said, "This is my first hot square since Deming. Maybe almost El Paso."

Leroy Keith smiled. "The grub is on the house on account of your long trip but the beer runs a nickel." He pointed to the bar with a single extended digit.

Jack patted his coat pockets and produced the dirtiest dime Leroy said he had ever seen. Jack and Shannon just chewed their folded tortillas and watched Leroy take a rag from his back pocket in an attempt to rub the dime clean. Jack waved him off. "Leroy, ye always hemmin' and hawin' since the damn Shakespeare days."

Leroy called over two cowboys from the end of the bar. They stumbled over and gave Jack a heavy slap on the back and introduced themselves to Shannon. Leroy tucked the dime into his pocket and strode to the fiddler, whistling the tune being spun and shaking his head. The cowboys were John Cox and the shorter Charles Shinn, both adorned in rough riding chaps and dirty white Stetsons fixed high off their brow, each a single action off the left hip. Cox wore an orange bandana. At times, he boasted the thing won in Mexico, playing poker, after scooping in some poor greenhorn his first time across the river.

Shinn said, "Jack, where ye been holed up? Have not seen the likes of you for some time now and where is that damn hat of yours?"

"Been haulin' water for Old Man Shelby down at his ranch. His water hole all dried up so the old boy had the company build him his own damn rail from the spring to his ranch. Well, he's too old to ride anymore so I'm lending a hand and he throws me some pay. Can't say no anyhow. Don't like to see horses die much even though if I never rode one again I'd be all apple pie. Had enough of them anyway. Two of his mares dried up and fell where they lay. The Brunn brothers hauled them off before the vultures got to them. Suppose they all butchered now and pass through some miners' guts sooner than later. Them fools wanted to take the knife to them right there. Shelby nearly caved one of their skulls in, I swear it. He damn near had a fit."

"Where does your hat come in?"

"Gittin' to it. After the tank filled and the horses watered, I made my way back here. Damn to hell got caught in that storm last night. Clean blew off my head. Never felt anything like it. Don't suspect I will again."

"And you didn't try to catch'er?"

"Hell no. If I did the Brunns be carting me off today. I'd place a dollar on it."

"So you ain't trying your hand at mining no more?"

"Hell, couldn't even tell ye what a pickax looks like."

Cox said, "Probably on account of the fact you didn't get much chance to use it. Old Jack dried up every claim in the district and then worked on drying up the whiskey at Grant's."

"That claim I never did bother arguing with."

The cowboys produced coin and Leroy Keith obliged with steady flow of drink. Shannon did not have to pry the cowboys for stories of adventure across the border or their days behind bars in Silver City, along with shouts concerning the bastard Deputy Hardin of this very burg. The charges of stealing cattle from across the border were not false, however, and John Cox confessed to the crossing and the days through Animas County and San Simon Valley. Leroy stood pouring drinks at the other end of the bar. He could do nothing but shake his head and insist that Cox's mouth would one day indeed get him in trouble. Leroy was not wrong.

Shinn fetched a grey and decrepit satchel from behind the bar. The buckles were gone but holding it tight were two thick hemp ropes neither frayed nor worn and the contents firm and sturdy within. In his drunken wonderment, he pulled a corked glass vial from an inside pouch and held it aloft for Jack and Shannon to marvel. The glass was cloudy. The light above exposed the greasy fingerprints upon the surface, displaying the frequency of past adoration.

Jack squinted. "There sand in there?"

"It is indeed sand. And while it's just sand in a country filled with sand and, believe you this, I have stepped on enough of the pulverized rock to fill a trip from here to eternity, this sand here is of unusual type."

Shannon sipped on a clear mescal. "Please, lad, please. Go on." Jack said nothing and stroked his beard in a puzzlement induced by the drink.

Shinn said, "This here sand is the very spot where Geronimo surrendered, boys."

Shannon said, "You don't say?"

John Cox nodded with great amazement and Shinn placed his flattened hand in the air and took oath on his mother. Leroy shook his head and said, "I heard this one before." He disappeared into a back room.

Shinn continued, "Pay no mind to Leroy. That day was the hottest since crossing back over the border and the herd had become restless. We nearly avoided stampede not soon after the last calf stepped out of the river. Considering our location and with the need to enter the territory, we talked it over and figured we had but one choice. And that choice was through Skeleton. Neither of us liked it at the time but didn't pay much mind to it. Just had to be done."

Jack said, "And did ye know when entering the particulars of the surrender?"

"In fact I did. Due to the papers in Denver." Shinn took a shot of the mescal and wiped his mouth with the back of his sleeve. "The beeves had begun to calm once we found shade along the trail. And not long after them rock formations did we come upon it. An apache blanket half dug up in the ground. The hairs on the back of my neck done stood straight as a board. I swear to my dear ma."

John Cox shook his head and then excused himself out the back door, which swung on two loose wooden hinges.

Jack said, "You done swore to her already."

Shinn continued, "Right there in the scrub. A cairn stood. I dropped my personals right there and hollered at John. We found camp for the night! John came riding up and didn't say a word. Just threw his leg over the horn and planted them on the ground. And let me tell you, that night. Not a sound in that canyon. Not a coyote, wolf, the horses, not a peep. Not even one of them monkey-faced owls I usually hear on that range. Hell, even the fire seemed to crack in half time. John just stared off into the stars and I couldn't do much of nothing either."

Shannon said, "On account of what you suppose?"

"Some Apache hex. Can't place it but that night I dreamed of Geronimo himself. He stood before me. Out on the horizon. I was small in his shadow and his face shone like the sun. I had to cover my eyes. In my dream I did just that. He raised his hands from around the earth and brought up with them mountains and the whole damn desert was running through his brown fingers. Kid you not. I woke in a dry sweat. Could not know what else to call it. My left hand gripping a fistful of desert. Hell. I just sat there staring at it and Cox thought I lost it. He's probably correct. I had this vial of chili powder I picked up in Sonora. Dumped it out and here you have it. The desert Geronimo put in my hand."

Jack said, "Well I'm stumped."

Shannon lit a cigarette. "A good luck charm is it?"

Charles Shinn glared into the vial. "If you mean like a rabbit's foot? Well, hell. Has not crossed my mind. My brother carried a rabbit's foot for years and trust me on this. Never did him an ounce good." Shinn palmed the vial and rolled it around in his hand. He then drew back his vest and slid the vessel into a deep pocket over his heart. He patted it before letting the vest fall back over his shirt. He said, "Pour another. That story makes my throat itch." His hand trembled. Jack obliged by filling a stumpy glass on the bar with mescal and Shinn made no haste.

Shinn said, "You suppose bad luck?"

"The sand?" Shannon asked and Shinn nodded.

"I would not suppose anything of the sort. And I for one have learned that hard lesson of the road. That one tends to make his own luck and when a man finds himself on a spot of earth, that man had indeed made a number of decisions for him to land there on that spot. To then suppose a force behind it. And then to suppose the force being malevolent or benevolent. You better pour me another, Jack." Shannon stopped and shrugged for he did not know where Shinn's mind was. Shinn nodded. Jack poured the drink and stroked his beard. Whether or not Jack was still stumped he did not say.

Cox emerged from the lingering darkness. He carried his bridle and advised Shinn to go off and secure his in the flop they were renting upstairs. Shinn did not argue with the request. He took another sip of the mescal and made his way off. He paused and turned to look at both Jack and Shannon. About his face was a twisted look as if his eyes were caught in the headlight of the local. He continued through the swinging back door. Shannon grabbed the top of his hat and adjusted its posture.

Jack said, "What is that about?"

"Search me."

"I've no intention to inquire. What do ye say, Shannon? Time to move on?"

After calling Leroy over to settle the deal, they wished him a quiet evening and Leroy could only hope their wish came true. Back into the night the men stepped. The street was still, with only the distant bark of a dog, crippled with mange, echoing down the street and summoning them forward. Shannon said, "Where to?"

"Won't do much good poking around for Connor this time of night."

"I agree. I agree." Shannon pushed his hat back. "Clear night."

Jack said, "That is why the Yanks flock here. Not to mention you tramps. This climate. Won't beat with a stick. I promise ye that. Anyhow, we sure as hell ain't going to be walking the streets looking for his ass. Too many drunks in this town. And I suspect Shinn comin' to ask you a few more questions."

"Me?"

"Yeah, you. That accent of yours makes you sound like ye gotta brain in that head."

"I can attest to a brain in this here head, my friend."

"Sure, can you attest to the size, I wonder?"

"Aye. Aye. Best be off now."

"Where to?"

"The depot. Suppose I'll be making my way."

"Wise beyond ye years."

Jack led Shannon past dark adobe walls and down a seamless wooden maze of back alleys, saloons, and gambling halls. A beggar called from a dark corner. From a window, raucous laughter transformed into a man screaming for his money back. They heard Spanish and muddled cursing beyond a battered wooden railing. Shannon put his hand on Jack's shoulder to stop him and left it there long enough to realize the voice was not Connor's.

Jack said, "Must have been that hop."

"Aye."

"He ever run off before?"

"No. Never." Shannon fastened the top button of his jacket to ward off the creeping chill.

"How long you been traveling with him?"

"Since Houston."

The moon cast protracted shadows across the square that led direct to the Arizona & New Mexico depot. They studied the depot from the far corner. A small creature skittered at the edge of the platform and beyond it the steaming giants lay still and cooling. Adjacent to the platform sat a regal train adorned with streamers and banners of greetings and congratulations. Small chains from the platform swung as if keeping time. Knocks and creaking could be heard from beyond the rails, lending to the suspicion that Hughes was about and a night as his guest would be imminent. Shannon agreed to wait until morning, when he could hop a departing train instead of bunkering down for the night in the cold.

Back to Wheat's Saloon, no clues as to the whereabouts of Connor, Fong or the Mexican boy could be found. A knock on the back door of Fong's Laundry went unanswered. Jack peeked through the side window. He saw no light to speak of. The night could offer no further answers and the question of boarding soon arose. Jack knew of shelter elsewhere in town and took Shannon toward their presumed last stop for the evening.

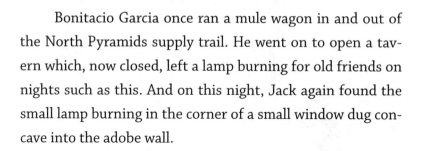

Bonitacio Garcia once ran a mule wagon in and out of the North Pyramids supply trail. He went on to open a tavern which, now closed, left a lamp burning for old friends on nights such as this. And on this night, Jack again found the small lamp burning in the corner of a small window dug concave into the adobe wall.

Jack knocked on the warped door. Chipped paint along the hinges crumbled off, catching in the splintered ends running down the edges of the boards. A small latch door drew back and closed. The bolt securing the door withdrew and Bonitacio greeted Jack with an embrace only a man as robust as he could offer. Shannon was welcomed inside and was shown a seat. Bonitacio took his hat and coat and poured water into an orange earthen cup. He placed it into Shannon's hands, which he emptied upon grasping.

Bonitacio smiled and said, "Tener sed." He tipped the olla to fill the cup again.

He showed Jack the detail of the olla recently traded for and explained its origins as being Apache. The age was not known. He lay upon all a gentle stare and his suspenders held his pants firmly over his belly. He ran a hand through his rough grey hair and then slowly faced an altar set on a makeshift table. There he lit a small candle, among other burning candles, under a rude portrait of Christ. Drawing the cross over his chest, he kissed his hands and looked to the heavens. His lips uttered an unheard prayer.

He grabbed his arm as if feeling a sharp pain and he fell back into a crude wooden chair, which did not betray his weight. Jack rushed and grabbed his shoulder to steady him. Shannon rose from his chair and stood frozen until Jack called for him to bring water. Bonitacio took a small sip from the vessel.

He whispered, "Gracias," again drawing his large, wrinkled hand through his hair and back down over his twisted face. "Francisco," he said.

Jack said, "Ye scaring me. What happened to Francisco?"

"Un muerto. Murdered."

Jack kept his hand on Bonitacio's shoulder and a distant rumble could be heard. The men's eyes shifted at the sound, none ever knowing if it was thunder or a late freight pulling into the depot. A cat slinked into the room from the small courtyard and jumped onto Bonitacio's lamp. He began to stroke the animal's head as the cat leaned into his curling fingers. Bonitacio smiled. He looked toward Shannon and then Jack.

"I am sorry," he said.

"It is us who is sorry, old friend."

Bonitacio sighed and demanded they stay the evening as his guests, as he wished not to be alone on this terrible night.

"Sit. Sit." He rose and placed a log on the simmering fire. From a low ligneous cupboard, he produced a corked jug and three squat glasses. He filled the glasses with a deep crimson wine that resembled blood. "California," he said.

The men raised and toasted his nephew and to his good memory. Each man drank the wine and Bonitacio filled again. "Sit, sit," he said. They sat to hear his story.

"A woman. A woman. And. Can you believe? His passion. His love. His guitar. His guitar led him to this place. Este lugar de la muerte. "

Jack rose and filled his glass again. "I know that boy loved that damn guitar."

"Si, si. Love will bring you to this place. Love and guitar. You remember Dundee mine? The camp? No recuerdo el nombre. Ah, si. The Eighty-Five. The Eighty-Five. Por favor?"

Bonitacio shook his glass and Jack obliged and motioned to Shannon, whose face was drawn and white. Shannon said, "I pass this round."

"Please, please there is more. The mine. Ten years old miner gave him guitar. From Tennessee it came. After explosion he gave. Por lo que recuerdo. I see him on the gurney and the two boys from far camp carry him. Le veo todavía dicen adios. With left hand. Left hand only. Other arm, you see? Dynamite. From Tennessee he came." The old man shifted his chair. The cat reappeared and landed on his lap. She curled to expose her belly. "Si, si," he said. "Francisco, he learn to play.

33

Slow. Oh, so slow. Would put my ears to my head! Dios, por favor. Detener la guitarra! Detener la guitarra! That boy. His mother, si? I made promise. I keep."

Shannon said, "His mother. Your sister?"

"Si. Mi Hermana. Maria fell ill not long after Franscico's third birthday. She no wake the morning of vernal equinox. That evening over her lifeless body. I swore. Te lo juré. I would care for the boy as if my own son. There on the wall a vigil to Christ. Like now. Si?" Bonitacio drew the cross and kissed his hand as he uttered yet another unknown prayer to the heavens.

"On wagon back to supply. Francisco would sit. Guitar wrapped in loin cloth. Envuelto como un bebé. Cradled and rocking. I would yell back, Francisco, play! Play! Every time he would play. Each time better. Then each time transform. You see. His fingers. Dominio de los corridos and his mind knew the melodies of the conquerors. Men older than I would stop and throw coin to him to play. Play he did. Of course, Fransisco became showman. An attraction at miner halls on weekend. Payroll was spent on women and liquor." Bonitacio laughed. "Las mujeres y licor. Soon he left supply trade and traveled among the camps. Among the towns. Along the rail. Sometimes alone and other times with second player. Others an accordion. Once being summoned to grand hacienda in the south. He play in the rancho style there. Praise, praise, he receive. His talents and name in demand. Mucho. Pero su corazón fue maldecido. Pero su corazón fue maldecido. A boy with no mother look for her in eye of every woman. You understand?"

Jack nodded, scratching his neck and he looked back at Shannon, who went to grab the hat that was not on his head. Shannon shrugged and emptied his glass. The cat, still curled in the lap of Bonitacio, lifted her head when the muffled sound of a wagon slowly passed.

"Como? On to another hacienda. To another camp where he would fall in love with another. Always searching. Never the right one. Always another's. Wife, daughter, si? Driven out of Sonora. Driven from the Pyramids. I tell him. I tell him. Yo le advirtió. He would wave his hand at old man. Yes, Uncle. Yes, Uncle. Never listen. One time I tell him. One time. Wrong man. Y así va. And what did happen? Night before last in the home of Herrara. He come home. He found him there. Playing guitar for wife. He took his ax and split his skull."

Jack leaned forward. "Tell me the law found the bastard?"

Bonitacio shook his head. "No. Not yet. God will be his judge now. Dios será su juez. They brought the guitar to me. Where else? Covered in blood. El color del corazón, si? I burned in there. In the back. There. In the flames it played. The wood splinter. Strings they snap. A sound came. Una sustantivo. Perhaps only in my mind. A song of the devil. A song for God. His song."

Bonitacio placed his hand on Jack's shoulder as he limped by. His leg stiff from years of hard trail. He took hold of the jug and shook it gently to hear the tumbling of the wine left inside.

"Room for more?" Both men nodded and Bonitacio served the three empty glasses. When finished, he placed the jug back on the small table and replaced the cork.

"Amor y destino." The three men lifted and drank.

Bonitacio unfolded two patterned blankets from a back room and laid them on the floor. Jack and Shannon offered gratitude and set in for the night. Jack curled and began to wheeze. Shannon dipped his hat over his eyes and saw Bonitacio sitting before the vigil. Shannon awoke sometime early that morning. Before drifting back off, he lifted his head to see the old man still there uttering some unknown and unheard prayer.

Darkness gave way to the forgiving morning light. Shannon awoke to Jack standing over him. Hand extended.

Shannon said, "Tell me you be an angel."

"Ain't that pretty."

Shannon dusted off his hat with two hard swipes. Bonitacio was gone. The chair stood an empty witness to the vigil. The candles were barely visible, with few omitting a trickle of flame. Shannon offered he may be out back and Jack confirmed he was not, his wagon and burro gone. On the table sat two bowls of cold beans, a small bottle of mescal and an apple. Shannon said, "I get the feeling we should say a prayer."

Jack nodded. "I'd remove my hat if I still had me one."

"We need to fix that one of these days."

On Railroad Avenue they approached the depot of the Southern Pacific. There was commotion by the dressed train. Men shaking hands in top hats and a fat man with a sash laughed as he was guided around the buffers by two skinny men, each in dark suit and cravat. Jack thought he had the fixings as the mayor of something. Women in green and yellow dress held umbrellas and congregated by the station, awaiting the departure of this celebration. An umbrella gently spun on the shoulder of one of the younger women. The patterns bled into one.

Shannon said, "Best not linger."

Jack nodded and spat. "Best not."

They walked down the line and stopped under a watering tower. Shannon turned and peered toward the soaring sun-stained clouds that stretched the horizon. Jack looked down and shook Shannon's outstretched hand.

Shannon said, "Many thanks. Sure do owe you one."

"You don't owe me nothing. I don't recall doing much. You would do the same whatever ye speaking of. Down the line. I reckon you will." Jack looked down and kicked the dirt. "Where you off to?"

Shannon turned and nodded west. "Out there, I suppose. Back that other way. Well, let's say it's past. And you?"

"The future done hold one thing. J.W. got the miner's friend. Gonna meet him for a few."

"Aye, working on another claim? Have one for me?"

"How does two sound?"

"I think you can manage, friend. So long."

"Adios."

Shannon passed under the water tower and searched for codes on the underside of the posts supporting the vessel. Seeing none he knocked twice on the wooden pole and made off toward a grove of trees to wait where the train goes slow.

Shannon ran his fingers over the prickle tops of the short grass as he squatted awaiting the westbound freight out of Lordsburg. Under young pecan trees and among scrub, he looked up and to the west. The cumulonimbus dissipated and grew outward, as if some unseen being were stretching them. He shifted and sat with his legs folded. He fumbled with rocks, throwing one at a scattering horned lizard in the bush. The sounds of pistons and valves gave him the cue. He again squatted. After the whistle blew, the freight moved down the line. He took a knee.

A shotgun blast exploded over the clamor of the freight and again the whistle blew. The train exhaled, coming to a stop.

Shannon lay on his belly. From afar, he could see the engineer and fireman jump down from the cab. Yells and cries came from down the line. More men could be heard screaming and running. Through the low brush he could make out blurred figures shifting. A wind shook through the pecan trees.

After some time the commotion died down. His thirst grew deep as the sun climbed to what he figured to be before noon. The depot was quiet going west; only eastbound locomotives bound for Deming and beyond came rattling in. He gained his footing and dusted off, making way down Railroad Avenue. As he approached the depot, he saw twenty or so tramps sitting lined up against a wall on the avenue. Two men with brown work shirts and rifles stood guard at each end of the line. The tramps sat stone stiff, a few sleeping and others with hats pulled over their eyes to shade from the sun.

A crowd gathered by one of the boxcars. What led Shannon there, he did not know, for his sense told him to flee but his feet betrayed the command. A man in a stained shirt sporting a Boss of the Plains eyed him wearily and yet Shannon could do nothing but move forward through the crowd. Over the shoulder of a man in a derby, he could see a tramp spread on the ground littered with buckshot through his vest. Blood saturated the grey suit with a deep crimson that only blood can shade.

A man on the far side of the encirclement said, "Damn fool pulled a revolver." The man displayed it.

Someone said, "When will they learn?" Shannon looked down at Connor, his blue eyes frozen, agape and glaring toward the heavens, reflecting like mirrors his ultimate destination. A skinny old man in a dark suit directed two teenage boys in aprons carrying a gurney.

"Get the leg, Oliver."

Connor was hoisted crudely upon the stretcher and the crowd parted. A woman gasped. Murmurs arose as the skinny man, the teenage boys, and what was Connor disappeared down the drag. Shannon followed only so far before veering left off the avenue. He came upon Wheat's Saloon like an apparition approaching its own grave. Gazing upon the facade, he adjusted his hat against the wind off the playa and stepped into the establishment. James Wheat stood holding a mug up to the light and he nodded to Shannon. He then looked over to the corner and nodded again. A chair drew across the wooden floor. Jack stood. "Howdy. Do my eyes deceive me? Ye looking like you in need of a jolt."

Shannon pressed against the bar and nodded to James Wheat, who left the bottle and two glasses on the bar. He retreated to the back. Jack grabbed the bottle and poured the clear liquor. Shannon twirled the beads that hugged the sides of the glass. He looked at Jack as they both threw back and slammed down. Jack poured another.

Jack said, "Don't tell me ye missed me?"

"Connor. He met his maker. At the depot."

"You seen him?"

"Seen him indeed. Buckshot. Nearly blew him in two. In two."

"What in the hell happened?"

"Tramps hopping a ride. Conductor tried to get them off. They say Connor pulled a revolver on them. Brakeman had a shotgun and fired." Shannon slammed the glass down on the table. "Another," he said.

"Was he heeled?"

"Heeled? No. Nor I. Robbed in El Paso, we was. Between here and Deming we never pulled the scratch together to replace the piece. Now. Now. I don't know."

"This is still no country for a man to be unarmed." Jack scratched his beard.

"Nor to be hatless."

James Wheat came back in with two plates in tow. He served beans and a loaf of sliced bread. Jack pushed the plate in front of Shannon. "Eat, eat, you'll be needing to get. This burg will be bloodthirsty. Lookin' for another killin' to drive all the hoboes out. The hunt will be on. Ye wanna tell me a brakeman has a shotgun at hand. Seen too much to believe that. J.W, what do you make of that?"

J.W. shook his head and what that meant they did not know. The back door was propped open by a large muddy rock and two crows picked in the cook fire. Shannon said, "Ask about Fong."

"J.W. You happen to seen Fong?"

"Not since day after last."

"And the Mexican boy?"

"No. Not him either. Why?"

"Oh, nothing. Probably nothing. Ye see'em. Tell me." Jack placed his hand on Shannon's shoulder. "Sure am sorry."

"Many thanks, friend. He was a decent man. He was. He was. Saved my life you know? Back in Sabinal. I had some jack after a harvest of oats. Waiting on a train and some yegg bums knocked me out in the jungle and evil bastards dragged me over the track. Sure they had a good laugh about it. Came to and there is Connor. Those blue eyes of his. Same grey suit. The one nearly cut in two. He had a cup in his hand. Old tin cup. Black on the outside from the cook fire. He put to my lips whiskey and water. An angel he was. My wits came rushing back and not one minute later, the freight came roaring down the line. It is I who should been two. Now him. There are two things that follow down that line, Jack. Death and your past."

James Wheat said, "Sad," and Jack nodded.

The food sat untouched and cold. They drank. Jack said, "What now?"

"Not many choices. One really. Ride on. Since Houston we rode together. Now, back to solo. The life of the tramp, Jack. No worries, lad. No worries."

Jack scratched the back of his neck and slammed down more of the spirit.

Shannon said, "Miner's friend?"

"Ain't no friend. Hell. To hell with it. You want company?"

Shannon raised his glass and after tipping the poison down his throat he coughed. "Jack, what are you getting at?"

"Company. Hell, I'm coming with you. Serious as all hell. Been here since eighty-two. No hat. No mines. No more damn horse. I'm sick of horses anyhow. Ye ain't got to water a train. Well, at least it's some other poor fool's job. And I'm sick of this damn town. I left Wichita all them years ago for adventure. Ended up Jack from Shakespeare. High time Jack shakes that off. Come now. We can share the women. We share the wine. I'm sure as hell up for it."

Shannon looked at James Wheat whose hands were flat on the bar. The rag draped over his shoulder fell off. He picked it up and swung it back over his shoulder and placed his hands on his hips, James Wheat said, "Is he serious?"

Shannon said, "I do believe he is."

"Hell. He is ain't he."

Jack poured J.W. a drink.

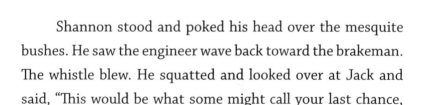

Shannon stood and poked his head over the mesquite bushes. He saw the engineer wave back toward the brakeman. The whistle blew. He squatted and looked over at Jack and said, "This would be what some might call your last chance, Jack."

"To hell with chance, just keep them eyeballs on that train."

Shannon ran his hands through the scrub. "You ever done this before?"

"If ye speaking of stealing a ride on a train. No. I done told you that already."

The sun simmered on the horizon and slid further west along the rim of the reducing landscape. The sky glowed with layers of sunset, painting the clouds adobe and brick. A warm shine colored the men auburn as they rose. Shannon said, "That is ours." A boxcar door passed wide open. Shannon gripped on to the grab iron, smacked his hand on the floor of the car and leaped. He stretched out to Jack, who on a trot, took his hand and the next moment found himself next to Shannon, sucking wind and laughing.

Shannon said, "The hard part's over, Jacky boy. Now you just sit back. Enjoy the scenery."

The train pulled slow through the depot, passing idle trains and boxcars filled with coke and fresh alfalfa from the Gila bend. Jack looked out on the wooden frames and ramshackle structures moving into his past. The wind picked up over his face. He closed his eyes. Jack looked back toward the depot and screamed, "I seen him!"

"Who?"

"There!"

Jack hung his head out the boxcar and pointed back down the line. Shannon followed suit.

Jack said, "There he is."

Shannon removed his hat and held tight to the edge of the car and said, "What in the hell is that boy doing?"

The Mexican boy was walking down the tracks. Headed west, out of town and into the desert. Over his shoulder, a gunny sack, loose with little in it. Shannon sat and inched back from the edge of the boxcar.

"What sense does that there make?"

Jack said, "I'm afraid it don't make none."

2: STEINS

Splinters of light dwarfed a distant framework of peaks, beams of sun expanding over ancient crags. Jack and Shannon sat and gazed at this sight. Jack rested his chin on his closed fist and he leaned into a stiff wind the train began to carry. Shannon pointed out toward the playa where veins of light reflected off what was left of the alkaline lake. Passing the clay and saltbush, the train shook birds foraging in that waste, sprinkling into the sky and dispersing down again over the playa. Jack closed his eyes and felt wind over his nose. His lids opened slowly to find dusk impeding the country. The steam whistle blew.

Shannon said, "The train is slowing."

"It is. Could only mean one place."

"That is?"

"Steins."

"You been?"

"Of course. Mighty good shot this train coming to a stop in Steins."

Shannon inched toward the edge and held tight on to his hat as he stuck his head out of the box.

"No lights? This Steins another burg?"

"Can't call it that. Mining stop. This box might fix to take on cargo."

"Best get off then. Bed down for the night."

"I recall some shacks in back of the main buildings. Abandoned usually. Sure to get cold up here."

"Aye, you know the way?"

Jack nodded.

As the train climbed out of the playa and up into the Peloncillo, a blue shadow fell on the expanse before them. The air took a chill and the slow speed of the train did not alter the bitterness of the wind that whipped into the empty boxcar. Shannon buttoned his overcoat. Jack followed suit, securing the filthy denim over his frame. The clanking of the tracks gave way to the whine of cylinders.

Shannon said, "Get ready to go on my word."

Jack spat. The darkness complete. The faint presence of light flashed between cars as the train pulled in. Freight filled with ore bound for El Paso stretched far over the pass. A deep blow of the whistle bounced off the towering rock walls surrounding the station. The iron beast slugged to a stop and the brakemen yelled down the line. Voices could be heard along with banging of doors.

Jack whispered, "What time you make it to be?"

"Nighttime. Hold still. Not a muscle."

The brakes hissed as some viper would and silence fell on the line.

Shannon turned to Jack. "Follow my lead. When we reach the clear. You show the steps."

"Agreed."

The endless lines of freight cars only offered one route to the town proper. Shannon led Jack beneath the gondolas, stopping once to wait on a brakeman walking past, who whistled as he swung a lantern at his side, the light dissipating into a cold air filled with smell of hard earth and sulfur. Under a final car, the men skittered on their haunches into a retention ditch. Two brakemen saw them from a distance but made no attempt to harangue the illegal fares other than to stretch a lantern toward the dark figures.

Jack said, "Them boys saw us."

"No matter. Keep moving."

The moon rose over Steins's peak. The night offered little cover as they emerged from the thick mesquite that guarded that section of track. Banging metal pierced the stillness of the mountain pass. Three men shoveled manure into a wagon. Each stopped as the travelers walked by. Frosted lights behind foggy windows decorated the evening and like beasts to a desert watering hole, they found themselves standing in front of a saloon. A Mexican leaned against a support beam on the porch. His hands stuck in his pockets. He smiled.

"Tobacco, por favor?"

Jack shrugged, "Ain't got none."

The Mexican stood grinning. They lingered on the porch.

Shannon said, "Looks rather lively. Shall we?"

"Let me see. Got some coin. Enough for drink here but liable to spend it all."

Shannon scratched the stubble showing on his check. He rubbed his hands together and blew. "We will have to worry about that later. Come on. I have a thirst to speak to."

Jack entered first. Few inside bothered to notice as the town grew accustomed to strange pilgrims down the iron highway. The beer presented was devoid of any palatable taste but it was stony and cleared dust from the throat. A corn whiskey was called for. Down it went bitter, with the impression of ethanol. They soon drew the attention of a Southern Pacific officer who walked over and leaned against the bar.

"Seen you men come in. The name's Paul. Thought you might answer a question for me. Do either of you happen to be aware of the penalty a man can face trespassing on company property?"

Shannon stood stiff, paying little attention. He glanced at Paul, gulped his liquor and blew the residue from his bottom lip. He wiped his face on his greasy sleeve.

Jack said, "As a matter of fact. We here are miners in from the Bachelor. Out of the Volcano district. Taking a break from the shafts to get a talking load on is all."

Paul eyed them and tipped his hat. As Paul stepped away the saloon keeper stood in front of them.

"Paul don't fancy your looks."

Jack said, "Nor I his."

The keeper smiled. He left, returning with two small bowls of a stew.

"You both can feed on this. After you scrape the bottom, I wish you both a good evening."

No haste was made disposing the contents of the bowls. After gathering themselves they walked out of the saloon. Paul looked after their exit and watched the men from the window in the door. Leaning against the post, the Mexican remained. He stuck his hand out and showed his palm.

"Tobacco?"

They skirted the saloon, walking further into a bevy of outbuildings. Jack pointed with his chin toward a row of ramshackle tin shelters outlining the boundary between supply and wilderness. Most dark. Some with the dim glow of candles inside. The last of the row black.

Shannon said, "This one."

Jack reached for the handle as the door swung open, knocking his hand away.

A voice ordered, "Step on back."

Into the moonlight appeared a shotgun pointed into Jack's face. The moon lent a silver sparkle to the firearm. The reflection ran a line down the barrel and outlined the face of their captor. The men shot their hands up with arms bent at the elbows.

Jack said, "What do you aim to do?"

"I aim to put a hole in you. Who sent ye?"

Shannon said, "Sent us?"

"Don't play me no fool, boy. I been expecting it. Like the Lords himself."

The men stood as if stone of the surrounding mountains. A coyote sounded in the distance. The man with the shotgun shifted his eyes.

"I said who sent ye?"

The coyote yelped again. The man stepped forward and with that motion he lowered the shotgun.

"Ya'll can lower ye hands."

Shannon slowly lowered his.

Jack said, "You ain't gonna point that thing in my face again?"

"No, sir. I give my word. I thought you were of red blood the both of you. The moon fools with my mind often. Now what in the hell do you think ye doing?"

"Looking for shelter. Last time I passed in these parts, I understood miners could find such here."

The man tilted his eyebrow. He gestured the barrel toward Shannon.

"And what do tell is ye story?"

"Don't have one. Looking for rest before the next train outta here."

"Well, hold on. Hold on now."

The man stepped backward and was again enveloped into the darkness from which he stepped. Jack motioned to Shannon. Shannon patted the air slightly and tucked the sides of his mouth down. Jack shrugged and spat. The interior of the tin hovel began to flicker. The man appeared back at the door shaking a match.

"Now my eyes tell me both ye white. Ya'll can thank him for ye shelter has appeared."

He then stepped back and cleared the doorway. Neither moved.

"Enter. Enter. Please. You are now my guests."

Shannon looked over at Jack and pushed him forward. The men entered slowly. The structure consisted of tin and was patched with planks where tin was no more, each board a different shade of rot and some with faded bills posted, a series of Chinese characters stamped in a crimson ink. Weather-beaten wood sat in a pile behind the door. In the corner, a filthy mat on top of which lay a tattered King James. The walls were adorned with crania of jackrabbit, rat, and lizards of all sizes. A gila skull with beads of dried corn strung from eye sockets. Strings of jawbones dangled from a whittled staff. Assorted teeth hung like tinsel off nails, rejoicing in some demented desert rite. Jack and Shannon stood above the man as he hunched over a misshapen iron box. There he lit a fire from a mix of mesquite and pion. As the flames rose he blew into the fire. The wood responded back with smoke. He rose reaching toward the ceiling and unhinged a small trapdoor.

"Helps with the smoke," he said and then gestured about the iron box. "Sit, ya'll. Come on now."

Both sat on what was nothing more than a cleared plot of desert, above which the shack was erected. The man poked at kindling with a thin iron bar and coughed. With the fire now revealing their surroundings, Jack and Shannon each could not point to the exact nature of the man's injury. The spark of the mesquite cast lines over the folds of skin, both aged and raw, that covered his face and neck. His hands had not escaped the same fate. He sat watching the fire, rocking and whispering something to it.

Jack said, "You mine?"

"Me, mine? Hell no."

"The rail?" Shannon offered, as he removed his hat and ran his soot-stained hands through his hair.

"Not a day. Lord, help us. If you have to know."

"We don't mean to impose," said Shannon.

"You sure as hell don't. Ended up with a shotgun in ye face."

The men did not respond.

"I was cowboy. I worked a nice size lot. Decent head of cattle. Just outside of Springerville it was. That was some time now. Years in fact."

The needles peeled off the piñon. The man added kindling to the fire, filling the shack with smoke.

"Damn hole," the man said, looking up.

No words were spoken for some time. All three just sat staring into the flame. Shannon began to doze and shook awake each time he did. Jack spat into the fire.

The man said, "Shelton. My name is Shelton."

"Howdy." Introductions passed.

"You want to know my occupation 'cause ye fixing to understand my face I reckon?"

Both men stared at Shelton over the flame.

"Can't hardly place blame on you. I myself would be itching for the story."

Shelton looked up at the hole and squinted to make out the stars above the high country.

"Was the cold coming on out there?"

Jack itched his head. "Yes, it was."

Shelton said, "Never can tell."

In the corner he bent over a covered bucket and removed the wooden plank that served as a lid. He dipped a tin can into the water and passed it to the men.

"Must work up a thirst on that rail."

Shannon parted his lips to speak but uttered nothing.

"I still recall the day. Clear as a mountain stream. Hot day on top of that. Out in the country riding all damn day. That particular day was particularly a dirty one. Roundup it was. Over some country God himself abandoned. I told myself that. I heard it in my mind. Not once neither and my time on this cold hard ground confirmed my suspicion. This roundup was a nasty time. Sun beating down and these damn beeves ain't cooperating and some jerky round noon got to me. Nearly shit my chaps climbing up and down off that damn stinking horse. Must have been thirty times. Finally rode in and boss said the roundup was off on account of matters in Holbrook. He was off to attend to business, so he waved that fat hand of his and said, 'Time off, boys,' and what else to do?

Me? No sir. I'm not tied to that damn ranch. I'm off to Show Low. Ain't a decent whore in Springerville or Eagarville for that matter.

"Sure. Long trip. Longer for the boss, as he would have to pay respects in Saint Johns before moving on to Holbrook. Now, the horse a good one, but I sure planned on a night in the country before making on to Show Low. And maybe my wits ain't about me but hell, damn if I thought much about it. Just went on with my business. The day was much like the last. This time, praise him, none of the damn runs. Round noon it was. I took a sleep and when I woke. That is when I felt it."

Shelton again poked the fire with the iron bar and stoked the coals underneath the piñon and arranged them flat.

"Ya'll still thirsty?"

"If ye pouring," said Jack.

Shannon raised his shoulders and scratched his forehead. Shelton dipped the cup again to serve his guests.

"Drink. Drink. No likker in this here shack, gentlemen. The Lord frowns upon it. More men died of damn whiskey in this country than in all the damn wars man created."

Shannon said, "So what did you feel?"

"Say what?"

"The story, man. The nap. You woke. What did you feel? What was it?"

"What was it? My gun."

"What happened to it?"

"It was missing. Gone. Didn't hear a damn thing. The bastards done took it right off me as I slept. Yup. Right then I didn't quite figure it but I jumped up. And still see that bastard's face. Cold as damn stone. Not a damn expression on that mug. His two partners up there on their horses. He just stood there right as rain with a damn piece of dry grass hanging out his mouth. With my firearm, yes, right in his damn hand. Me? Tell you right. Felt naked as day before that damn savage."

Shannon said, "Who the hell was it?"

"No other than the Kid himself."

"And who would that be?"

"The damn Kid!"

Jack said, "Hold on now, Shelton. He's not from these parts. The Kid being the Apache kid. A renegade."

"Aye, a rogue was he?"

Shelton leaned forward, "A renegade? A rogue? A goddamn murdering heathen bastard."

Jack said, "You was sure it was him?"

"No guessing on my part. His part neither. What the bastard was sure of was, he knew, I knew who he was. What could I do? I threw up my hands. He come over and tie my hands up. Me? I just spat. What else could I do? They boosted me on the horse and put a hood over my head. Could not see a damn thing. Burlap it was. Smelled like gunpowder. Just damn awful in that sun. Hell, it was gentlemen. Hell. The first day. The worst. That sun. That terrain. They took me up in the Whites. Got colder and colder and we just kept climbing and climbing. Damn near fell off the horse cannot tell you how many times. They had enough sense to tie my hands in front of me. Shit. Held that saddle for dear life. Horrifying. Didn't know if some poor fool would happen on my bones up in them godforsaken hills. Not one of them spoke damn lick of tongue. Hours on end. None of them even coughed. And finally they pulled down and sat me against a rock. After a while they removed the hood. They took off my boots at least. I'll give that to them. There's some decency in the heathen mind."

Shelton banged the rod beside the box, summoning ash and sparks from the coals. He watched the sparks rise out of the hole and continued.

"They passed javelin round and water. I didn't look at them much. I collapsed into sleep. One of them brought water over and shook me awake. Gave me a mighty gulp. I coughed my throat was so damn dry. The Kid got a good laugh out of that one. I heard him speak and next thing I know the bastard kicked me and said, 'Time to ride.' I just looked up in them black eyes of his and spat. What could I do? This went on for days. Watered me. Fed me. Drove the damn horse. Down valley, over river, grassland, scrub, desert, stone. Just saw the country. The land out the bottom of that damn sack. That damn grimy sack.

"Days. Nights at the fire. I figured I'd be skinned and fed to vultures. That fate began to make perfect sense after God knows how many days on that saddle. It was indeed torture. The Kid knew it. He done been on enough trails to know. Enough rides to hell to be damn sure of it. He knew. Night before the last he came up to me at the fire. Kneeled in front of me. Did not say shit. 'Cause, funny, the bastard speaks perfect English. Still not a word. Just knelt there in front of me. Me? I just spat. What could I do? I told him to go to hell. He got up and walked into the darkness. Don't take the King of France to figure that one. I hoped for a quick end. Fed me deer that night. Damn good. Even took off the rope round my wrists. I ate like a dead man. Never had deer before. Never since neither.

"We came to a stop the next morning. Off the horse I went. Took the sack off my head and folded the thing. Grubbiest sack you ever seen. They kept it. Don't wonder why. There ain't an answer. The sun was just starting to climb. We was at the base of some mountain range unfamiliar to me then. Now? Well. The Kid climbed down off his horse and without saying nothing they stripped me naked. What could I do? I spat. Just as I spit now. There I am. Stark naked in front of these three heathen Apache and the Kid says, here is what he says, he says, 'Start walking.' And he points the way and compels me with my own damn pistol. What could I do?"

"You spat?"

"Hell no. I started walking. That is what I did. I could have been in the center of hell. I was in fact. No idea where the hell I was. Middle of goddamn nowhere. Stark mad naked as Adam in the Garden. I turned back and there they was. A distance but there watching. Sick bastards. The sun. The damn sun. I never did curse it. God compels it to rise as it does. I trusted he would take me. I half expected for them to fire upon me. Delirium. A poisoned mind. Cannot know if my mind was gone but I came over a hill and stepped through about, well must a been hundreds of hares just staring at me. I looked back and saw hares. Hundreds of them. No Kid though. I suspected a fast end by rifle but was none but fantasy. I walked on. Stumbled. Lurched. How long? Well. God knows.

"Came to and there was a white man standing over me. Thought he was Gabriel himself. I reached up and touched his beard. He said, 'Sargent, he's alive.' That I was. Alive. By the grace of God. I found him in that there desert."

Shelton pointed out beyond the confines of the shed and then rose and carried back a piece of what he said was hare. Rough cut on the bone with pieces of fur uncleaned on the meat. He placed them bare on the coals. A method he learned on the trail. Shelton continued.

"The soldier was from Fort Bowie on patrol. Funny thing about it was, he later said he never been in that stretch of wilderness before. His horse just drifted down the very wash I lay and he didn't protest the animal's wishes. And I swear to you, when he put his canteen to my lips. The pain it produced.

You wouldn't believe. Much like needles down my throat. He carried me quite a ways I suppose and then two soldiers were carrying me. I awoke in white sun. Sat up and a dozen soldiers sat up in their bunks. It was the barracks. Soldiers in their skivvies and such. A doctor from Tennessee worked on me. Saw me fit. Most of my skin much like my face. The Doc said worst case of sunburn he ever saw. Swore to it in front of the lieutenant. Lay there for two weeks and the soldiers, God bless them, would come sit by my bunk. Tell me of running down the savage. Men they was. Men.

"I came to learn there was Apache at the fort after I left. Enough sense they had. I would have cut the bastards down myself. Wouldn't have paid the rules any mind. Anyhow, they sent me off shaved, dressed, armed and saddled. Was I afraid? Hell no. I wanted them bastards to show their red faces. Especially the Kid. The soldiers pointed the horse toward Steins and here I sit today. Still burning the lamp waiting on my chance to kill the Kid. Just the chance mind you. Don't think for a moment that's a result of not trying. Been plenty to do since Bowie closed, you know? Took up with Thacker, Williams and Slaughter. Fine men all. After the Merrill tragedy and the massacre of them Germans, I took up with the First as an irregular. No official will swear to it but ye damn sure there I was. They came through here and you didn't even have to ask ole Shelton. There I was. Ready to take on the heathen."

Shelton plucked the hare off the coals with a long sharp stick and in turn passed the game round.

"Tough," he said before biting down on the charred meat.

Jack and Shannon made little sound other than the chew of muscle and cartilage. The coals now were little speckles of orange stars and the shadows crept back into the corners of the shack. Jack called for more fuel on the dying heat. Shelton obliged.

"Ain't much left after this rekindling."

Jack said, "No matter. Best we get warm."

Shelton prodded the growing flames and continued. "Yes. Yes. Yes. I have also heard of the Kid meeting his end on more than one occasion but I don't believe it. I ain't seen his body. Perhaps never will. Tell you what. I won't believe it until these two eyes set upon his two. Then I'll raise my hand and swear to the Almighty.

"One occasion found me and a small posse up round Globe and San Carlos. That was prime grounds for the Kid. He knows that country like none other. We were following the Black River, skirting some terrible mountain that hid what, God only knows. For days we are following a trail of what we think is Indian. We come round and pointed south toward Globe and not all far from where the Merrills meet their slaughter, we came on what you might call some pool of death. We dipped into a wash and there it was. The water from some past rain remained. Holding due to the shade of outcroppings above. Hell, it was. Decay.

"The bodies were piled. Must have been twenty or so. Multiple states of decay in this puddle. Men, women, children, all ages. Oh God, the smell. The smell. One old boy in the posse started crying and if it was from the stench or the realization of the deplorable state of humanity, we did not ask. For it was. We wasn't the first through. A cross stood erect above it a short ways. Marking this place of slaughter and evil. We knelt in prayer and moved on. Reaching Globe, we disbanded. Not a man who laid eyes on that horror could have walked away unaffected.

"I sat over a whiskey and inquired about the site. None knew except this large, haunted fellow who spoke up. He told me the site was not one murder but many over time. Mexican, savage, and Christian. All died there and all committed evil deeds in return on that ground. Funny thing was, I went out to the pisser, came back, he was gone. Except the bartender said the man brought my next four rounds. Hell. What to do except paint my nose? So I did. After Globe I came back to Steins and here I sit. Here you sit."

Jack said, "Do you still hunt the Kid?"

"In my mind. In my mind. I knows he here. Not down in Mexico or up in the Sierra, like they say or dead as some cowboys claim. Like I said, no one collected on the bounty and no right man ever turned in the corpse. He's out there and I'll have my day. Lord as witness."

The fire was no more. The glowing coals hummed and faded into darkness.

Shelton said, "Best make the spot you fix to sleep in."

Shannon counted the bones pegged on the wall. He fell asleep after forty-seven. It was still dark when Shannon woke. He found Shelton fiddling with the firebox.

Shannon looked up at the covered hole. "Is the sun up?"

"No, not yet. Best make it down to the depot before sunrise."

Shannon nudged Jack. He raised his head and rubbed his left eye.

Shannon said, "Come dawn the yards will be crawling with bulls. Best move on."

By the grainy light of a miner's lamp, they collected themselves and bid Shelton farewell. He passed the tin cup once more.

"When you get on to Californy make sure the ocean is still there for me. Mind it now. Mind it. And for God's sake don't get off the damn train between stations. Even though Geronimo and his kind is locked up, don't mean there ain't some savages roaming this country."

Jack waved and Shannon tipped his hat. They turned to face twilight.

The line through Steins Pass remained end-to-end freight. A steady metallic banging could still be heard and coal was pungent in the air. Jack pointed out a group of men unloading a car down the line. Shannon led Jack down a high fence away from the commotion. Coming upon a hole in the fence, they crawled through and were among barrels and freight of all sizes. High piles of ore lined the back of the yard. Shovels dug into the side stood straight and abandoned after the shift ended.

They watched the twilight fade brighter into the beginnings of dawn as piles of minerals around them caught the glimmer of commencement. A door creaked open, slowly squeaking shut. The shuffle of footfall followed. Shannon patted Jack's arm and both men deposited themselves behind a pile of broken earth. Hull, the watchman, came to walk his rounds. Shannon put his finger to his lips and he pointed toward Hull. Hull stopped in the middle of the yard and bent to inspect something. Shannon leaned into the pile. His eyes still. Aware. Jack held his breath and went to grab on to Shannon, before pulling back his hand. Shannon removed his hat and placed it gently on Jack's head. Without further signal Shannon crept around the heap. Jack's eyes widened watching Shannon disappear from sight.

What Jack heard next was a groan, struggle, and silence. The sound of dragging followed. The scraping of metal on rock caused Jack to straighten. He put his hands back on his knees. The corner of his mouth twitched. Six chimes of a steam whistle blew. The door creaked again and Shannon came around the side of the pile and grabbed the hat off Jack's head.

"C'mon! We catch this ride. Hustle now."

They ran across the yard and toward the door from which Hull came. Jack saw nothing as he glanced to the spot where Hull must have stood.

Jack said, "What we going to come up on through that door?"

"It's clear. Come on."

The iron beast began to moan. Sliding rods and pistons. Wheels caught sand. Again, the whistle chimed.

"Come on!"

Shannon threw a sure grip on the grab iron and with two steps pulled himself into the car. He turned to watch Jack catch up. They locked arms. Shannon growled and hoisted Jack up into the car. On the opposite track, a man standing on top of a train spotted them. He wore a filthy top hat and held a small dog. As they passed, the man shook his head at the tramps stealing a ride out of that mountain pass. The train eased past the towering rock wall to the north. Jack looked back at the conical peaks of the crest line and caught his breath on all fours.

"What in the hell happened back there?"

Shannon crawled into the shadows of the car and outstretched his legs. His boots could only been seen by a slither of light.

"I jumped him. I jumped him, Jack. That's what the hell happened."

Jack stood and walked over to Shannon, wobbling as he strode.

"And what do tell do ye mean by that?"

Shannon dug into his pocket and unfolded his hand. "Took his rings. And let me see. Four bucks in change. Ain't that something? Heaven sent. Heaven sent."

"Why did you go and do that?"

"How did you gather we would eat down this line? I don't go begging at back doors, Jack. No. Don't lose sleep on it though. You'll share in the bounty."

"And the watchman? What came of him?"

"Poor lad has worries no more, Jack. No more."

"You killed him?"

Shannon stared back.

Jack clicked his tongue. "You care to answer?"

"I stuck him. Happy?"

"Happy? Hell No. You killed a man in cold blood. A working man done us no harm. Might as well of been me."

"You? Jack? Come now. It's over."

Jack spun toward the open door. His beard itched and he stood peering into the rising sun. The train began the down grade from the Peloncillo into the valley of San Simon. A vast expanse lay under him outlined by the dark horizon of Chiricahua. The infinite contours of wind spun clouds responding to that vista and the currents of energy there. Jack lost in this scene. His stare held true to a soul wandering in this unforgiving wilderness of misplaced souls. A sheet of metal came from under the train and scraped along the tracks. His trance broken, he fixed on the rocks and bare ocotillo speeding by in a dense haze, jarring to the cadence of the rails.

Jack said, "We ain't gonna kill no more."

"Come again?"

"We ain't gonna kill no more," Jack yelled over the racket. "Not while ye with me. You hear?"

"Aye. I hear."

"What's to say they ain't gonna be waiting on some damn hoboes the next station?"

"Nothing says it. Nothing says it, Jack. But they will not be. He will not be found for some times. Perhaps days."

"I ain't even gonna ask. I ain't even gonna ask."

Jack put his back against the wall of the train and propped the back of his head on the thick lumber of the boxcar. He began to drift and woke suddenly in a sweat. Shannon was no longer on the far side of the car. Removed now from the shadows, he stood next to the open door. A solid figure against the backdrop of blur.

"Maybe a stop up ahead."

Jack answered, "How long I been asleep?"

"Five minutes."

"Five minutes? Hell, stopping already?"

"We've slowed. Slowing more now. Be ready, Jack."

"Damn it all. Damn it all to hell." Jack got up.

"There will be time for that."

Jack braced himself against the wall beside Shannon.

"If we have to make a jump. Follow my lead."

Jack ran his hand through his matted hair and spat.

"Oh, Lord. What all do you see?"

Shannan said, "Cattle."

There on the plain grazed three hundred head of the beasts, some watching the train roll by, most chewing head down on the Chihuahuan scrub, reaching from the scorched sand and gravel. The whistle then did sound a short cadence of blows.

Shannon said, "Brace yourself now."

The train rolled through a small station along the Southern Pacific line.

Jack said, "Where is we?"

Men could be seen around a watering well, fed by pipe, flowing with glittering and clear water. Cattle mulled around the swallow pool. A man on a porch sat rocking in a chair with two blonde children on his lap. He stopped his sway and studied the train. One of the children waved. Shannon waved back, not knowing what gender the child was. A man in all white took off his wide-brimmed hat and held it aloft at the passing travelers.

Shannon said, "Friendly."

"I guess we ain't stopping?"

The train passed women in deep-red shawls with diamond patterns. They carried woven baskets filled with folded blankets. Jack thought they might be headed to a small adobe church that quickly faded into the distance.

"Good folk," Jack said. "Good folk."

And the train rolled on, leaving those passed frozen in the moments seen by the travelers. The car smelled of carbonate. A wind again blew through the car. Sitting in the sun, the men inspected their possibles. Shannon reached into his inside coat pocket. He wiped the blood off of his knife with spit from his fingers and ran the side of the blade into his dark pants. Jack looked on. To the south, the plain stretched toward the impression of mountains. Leading there were riparian strips, blended with blooms like passageways into the panorama of dark wilds. Leading to a promise that somewhere up there, a man could find a purpose beyond this one.

Shannon removed the apple from his coat pocket. The one left to them by Bontacio, back in that frozen time.

Jack spat. Shannon drew the blade through the apple and handed Jack half. Jack held it in his hand staring at the fruit.

"No appetite, Jack?"

Jack looked at Shannon. The apple was crisp, white and where the skin met the flesh, an outline of red, where Shannon cut with the blade.

Shannon said, "I'll eat it if you're not hungry." Jack rubbed the flesh on his shirt and inspected the meal. Jack bit the apple.

3: BOWIE

Rolling stock was at standstill down the track and the train found place in line. Brakemen were inspecting pistons under a lumber car, when the men hopped off undetected. Down the embankment they slid into a dry irrigation ditch, where they sat in near silence. The sound of a wind in the distance could be heard. Shannon inspected the horizon and said, "We're still sitting in this valley. It must meet an end some-where. Everything does." Brakemen moved their inspection down the track and Jack and Shannon moved on, stepping into a depression cut from seasonal floods. Shannon dug into his jacket pocket and produced the two rings he slid from the watchman's fingers. Shannon held them in his palm and rocked his hand in such a way to observe the sun reflect off the rings.

Jack said, "What do you aim to do with them?"

Shannon leaned over and dug a shallow hole. He placed the rings in and covered them with sand.

"I can tell you, I don't aim to get fingered with them on me. I am headed into town, Jack. You're welcome to join unless you plan on eating sand."

"You going to remember where ye buried them things?"

Shannon looked at Jack and stood. "That train still hasn't budged?"

Through low scrub they walked toward outcropping buildings that peeked over the horizon and stood separated from the depot and the main stretch of town. As they drew closer, a man on horseback approached. The rider stopped some distance away, turned back toward the town and rode on. They came to a wash and stumbled on a blackened firepit. Three cans lined a dead mesquite along with two wooden crates, a third smashed for kindling.

Shannon said, "A jungle."

"A what now?"

"No matter," Shannon said. "We will come round this away again."

Shannon circled the area and studied the surroundings, scrub, rock, and endless jagged range encircling them. Jack kicked over one of the cans. Sand poured out. Jack picked up the can and dropped it after smelling the inside. Shannon searched the horizon. Jack said, "*The Liberal* had them an article once on the moon and the particulars of such. Men who worry about those matters, seemed to think this country here may resemble what is all up on that rock. Hell, looking out on it here. We all could be on the damn moon. If ye told me that. I wouldn't fuss." Shannon tossed a rock. Clouds of sand drifted off in the vanishing point between mountain and desert floor. They moved on.

They steered away from the depot, which jostled with passengers and livestock in the haze of the early noon. Reaching the gray structures, only litter gave clue of human activity among the assemblage. A sign read Mercantile and pointed toward the depot. The faded bill on the other end of the facade showed "OO." Jack said, "A good a place as any from the looks of it." The atmosphere inside was dry, dark and no souls occupied the bar or tables. Pictures of local cowboys and ranchers hung framed on the walls. Jack and Shannon bellied up to a short bar with blue and white tile on the surface. At one end sat two barrels circled by dull iron hoops.

Jack said, "I'm catching a nose of something."

"Aye."

A short Mexican woman appeared from a side doorway above which a portrait of George Bowie hung. She stopped and turned upon seeing them at the bar. Shannon said, "What in the hell is going on here?" They stood erect with eyes trained on that doorway. She soon entered with two bowls. She wore a checkered apron and bore no expression. Her dark skin showed no lines, as if she had worn the very same one her entire life. She served black beans, brown water and white liquor drawn from the barrels and each burned as it went down. The beans were cold with a thin film over the surface. Shannon threw down coin and she gathered her fee and returned to the side door.

They stood over their empty bowls. Jack picked his teeth with a splinter he snapped from one of the barrels. Shannon collected the glasses and poured in each another round of the liquor. They stood in silence and felt the burn of desert sun on their skin. Jack raised his eyebrows after his last gulp. He looked at the dust-covered tables surrounding them and said, "Ye think this place sees business?" Shannon shrugged and made for the door.

Jack looked toward the back door and said, "Gracias, ma'am," and followed Shannon out.

Shannon walked ahead of Jack and their shadows became them as they stepped down the cracked clay street, bordered by desert. The haze vanished and they could see trains had cleared. A trail of black smoke heading west signaled the departure of yet another. The man on horseback reappeared as they rounded the corner. He tipped his hat. He wore a white buttoned coat, the lapels outlined in red. His boots shone and he wore a mustache combed and prominent under his nose.

"Good afternoon, gentlemen."

"Afternoon," Jack said, squinting up at the horseman. "How are ye?"

"Just fine. Fine indeed."

Shannon said, "What can we do for you?"

"That was certainly what I aimed to inquire about. Are you gentlemen looking for work?"

"What kind of work would that be?"

"Harvesting. Plenty of berries to pick for an enterprising man."

"Here?"

"Yes, sir. Just yonder." The man pointed and Jack and Shannon both looked. "This here is the bottom of the valley. Six wide miles of irrigation in these parts. My brother has small acreage up the valley where the Cienega runs through but half a mile north of here is my plot." The man spat. "So, what say you?"

Jack looked at Shannon and looked at the man.

Shannon said, "Sorry. We're not looking for work."

"Not looking for work?" The man sat erect on the horse and spat.

"What can I ask your business is in this town?"

"Just passing through."

The horse snorted. "I see. Tramps. Damn lazy tramps. I can inform you gentlemen that we do not take to your species in this valley. We got enough trouble. I recommend you move along now and to be clear with you, I will inform the sheriff of your presence."

Jack turned. "Come on, Shannon."

Shannon stood and stared at the man.

The horse jostled and the man said, "Wipe that evil stare off your face. Now go. Go."

Jack grabbed Shannon's arm. "I said, come on."

Shannon flung his hand off.

"I'm coming. And a good day to you."

The man spat and watched Shannon and Jack make way back into the desert scrub from which they came. Down into the wash and back to the jungle, where a hobo sat on a crate poking a charred stick at the slumbering fire. He wore a straw hat, frayed at the edges and a work shirt, his dungarees ripped at the left knee. "Howdy," he said when they approached.

"Howdy," Jack replied.

The two squatted around the firepit and the hobo asked if either had any tobacco. Both had none. The hobo tipped his hat toward the sky and said, "Where you off to?"

"Down the line," Jack said. "Willcox, I figure. It's the next stop anyhow."

"You?"

"Same. Same. Fruit tamping. Pick up some work there and on to California. Up to Salinas for the season."

Shannon threw a stick and said, "You find work in this burg here?"

"Yes, sir. Did you happen to have a run-in with the sheriff?"

"No. Just his lackey."

The hobo took his hat off and fanned his face. "No wind today," he said. "Must have been one of the Fernandez brothers. I can tell you they don't take to bums, as they say, in this country. Not enough hands to pick and as soon as the hoboes come railroading down the SP. You either picking or in the box on a vag count and when you get in front of the judge, he's liable to set you picking anyhow. Have you done a share of picking?"

Shannon removed his hat and ran his hands around the rim. He looked at his hand and rubbed the dirt from his fingertips. "Aye, did my share of chopping through Texas. I can attest to that. I didn't take to it much but I earned enough to move on. And now. And now." Shannon placed the hat back on his head and stood. "You know of red ball off to Willcox?"

The hobo stood and over his brow he placed his hand to make out the distance. "Down that way should sit one," he said. "I was fixing on making my way over. Now that commotion died down, it should be no trouble hopping on."

Jack said, "Trouble?"

The hobo sat back on his heels and continued to wave his hat. "I can tell you I stood witness to the incident. I was there just wandering through the station. Sheriff knows I've been working the field, so. The train loaded and passengers were mulling around. The whistle blew. I cannot say what the Lord had planned. Something awful it was. We all, and I mean every man, woman, child, looked toward the back of that train. Hell, even the engineer had his head out the cab with his jaw agape. There in his full uniform was a soldier. Just as lying down to a nap in the sun, he put himself across the rail, under one of the cars. If I told you time froze, I would beg you to believe me.

"The conductor yelled to the engineer to apply the brake. But every poor soul witnessing this sad event knew, we're all about to see this soldier cut in two. The wheel rolled and what a funny world this is. Before the wheel turned onto his body, you know what all happened?" The hobo looked at Jack.

Jack said, "What all happened?"

"I'll tell you, friend. The damn brake beam struck him with such force it threw him off the track just as the wheel came down on him. The entire lot of us just gasped at the miracle and shock of it. The train stopped. And the soldier? He just got up. All he suffered was a ripped jacket. He looked down at all of us and turned and walked off as if the whole lot of it hadn't happened. He spoke not a word. The conductor stuck his head back in his perch, blew the whistle and train was off. No one even walked after the poor fool. We was all still frozen. Some man said he must have been back from the Philippines. Any soldier who escapes with his life from that hell pays with his mind." The man shook his head. "Yes. Yes. Funny world. Don't make a lick of sense does it?"

Jack said, "I can confirm it don't. I can swear to it."

The hobo nodded and Shannon said, "I will be back. Wait here, the both of you."

Shannon walked a short ways and disappeared into a depression and emerged the other side. He studied the lay and knelt, his movements concealed by scrub. The hobo watched him and looked at Jack. Shannon returned through the brush. "Now where be that red ball?"

The hobo said, "Follow me then." The three crossed the tracks.

4: WILLCOX

The train rumbled slowly west and the hobo nodded off. Jack and Shannon sat in the silence between them and regarded the basin. Buttes rising out of the loam sat in bare landscape like markers for some unknown eon. Volcanic ridges outlined the horizon with pine timber blanketing sloping granite. The sun cast deep shadows where canyons ran veins into the heart of those outlying barriers.

The train slowed and then whined to a stop. The hobo said, "Jump off here," and one by one, they did. The hobo led them to another jungle, where he would be parting ways. Off to the peach groves, as he didn't want much to do with town. A well-stacked fire with coals sat smoking in the camp but the jungle was empty. "Must have just hopped on," the hobo said. "You fellas been to Willcox before?"

Jack said, "No but heard plenty."

"Don't know what you heard but fair warning. Watch yourself. Some bad men make home in them saloons. Stay out of the west side and you'll do just fine." The hobo extended his hand and both Jack and Shannon returned the gesture. The men watched him fade into the approaching dusk, growing purple in that early desert evening.

The sun faded under the horizon and running east on Railroad Avenue, Jack and Shannon shuffled their feet wearily. The journey from New Mexico and events at Steins, that very morning, began to feel as if some queer dream, lost in a hot summer nap. The drag was wide and every few feet they stepped sideways to avoid piles of manure that littered the road. Horses were tied at every storefront and men gathered along the redwood depot in their suits, talking the day's business and watched arrivals as they stepped down off trains. Children ran in circles giggling as Jack and Shannon passed. A dog barked and followed them with a beastly stare, until the animal was called off and ran back inside the mercantile. Shannon stopped a miner going the opposite way. The man was drunk.

Shannon said, "Where abouts is the west side of this burg?"

"That away." The miner pointed and smiled.

Jack said, "Didn't that rambler back there advise against the west side?"

"Aye. Where else to pawn these rings and go booze blind?"

Jack shook his head. "Boy, we in for it. Ain't we?"

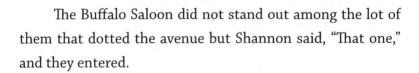

The Buffalo Saloon did not stand out among the lot of them that dotted the avenue but Shannon said, "That one," and they entered.

The clamor from the card tables held the attention of every man standing tall or slouched in that place. The proprietor exclaimed, "Another winner," and told the unwashed and tattered gathering to drink up and they obeyed.

Jack rested his head on the bar after throwing down a gulp of whiskey that carried the smell of creosote and mouth of tobacco. Shannon said, "Suppose I try my luck?"

Jack said, "Didn't take you as a gambling man."

"Oh, I have had my share of luck, Jack and most of it bad. Bound to turn around for me."

Jack shook his glass and with the whiskey again full said, "Bound to turn for every man, Shannon. Problem generally, ye never know when it's coming."

Shannon drank.

Jack stretched his neck. "What's the game?"

Shannon said, "Faro."

"Faro? You have to be a snake or a fool to play that game. Not one man don't know it's fixed. I can tell you that game will be banned in this territory one day. Ought to be a law."

"Snakes and fools, Jack. I like those odds."

"Don't lose all the damn money. Remember our bargain."

"It is burned, Jack. It is burned. Now wish me luck."

Jack raised his glass. "Ye need it." He drank.

Shannon made his way to the table.

On an empty stomach, the rotgut began to take hold. Jack looked in the mirror behind the bar to see a disheveled and bearded man staring back at him. The whites of his eyes held the only clue that the beast be mammalian in that reflection. He ran his hand over his face and turned when the crowd erupted with cheer. Jack said, "Fool," and he shook his head and looked into his glass. Frantic cheers came from behind and a tossed hat hit him in the back of his neck. "What in the hell?"

"Big winner over there I suppose," said the barman, filling Jack's glass.

Jack sipped his whiskey and before him emerging from the crowd came Shannon, with two drunks hanging round his neck as if baboons. Shannon announced, "Barkeep! Every man a whiskey!" The cowpunchers, railroaders, and a slew of miners, all drunk, threw up their wares and put forth their glasses with the proprietor and barman pouring frantically. The proprietor called over the fuss, "Keep playing and drinking, gentlemen! Luck is in this here establishment." They toasted to an unnamed lady, as there was none about, and threw up another hooray.

84

Shannon turned to Jack. "Jacky boy! Ye of little faith. Little faith."

"I'll be damned."

"You are, dear friend. Tonight we dine on oysters and pearls."

Jack scratched his head and smiled. "Where to?"

"Aye, the honky-tonk. But first. Some overdue business."

Jack sat on the stoop of a mercantile waiting for Shannon. Slightly rocking in that cool desert night, he watched hacks pass at a gallop and men strolling with thick black cigars and clouds of smoke trailing. Chinese laborers hurried down the side street, carrying short lamps and sacks thrown over shoulder. He was almost drunk and was staring at the bright high moon, when a hat fell on his head. He stood and grabbed at the thing. "What the?"

Shannon stood behind him. "Come on now, lad. Let me see it on you. Does she fit?"

"Hell," Jack said.

"Come on. On your head. On your head."

Jack went to the mercantile window and put the hat on. He grabbed the brim and pushed it tight around his forehead. Shannon said, "Well? Come on, Jack. Never took you as shy."

"You didn't have to buy me a hat."

"That there is peculiar thank you but I shall find it sufficient from a ruffian of your ilk." Shannon put his arm around Jack's shoulder. "We'll purchase some fresh after the evening's celebration. Now, lad, the ladies of the night await." Back to the street and laughter and before long, ladies with painted cheeks and gaudy wears beckoned them into the hurdy-gurdy. A tall mustachioed man in tight white shirt and black vest introduced himself as Robert Screed, proprietor, and immediately showed the two to a table cloaked with thick red cloth.

On the far end of the room a fiddler stood on a low-rising stage. His hat barely on his head and he wore a white ruffled shirt with yellow trim as if in a Kentucky wedding. The fiddler yelled, "Gentlemen, find yourself a partner for the next dance." The second fiddler then stood and the bar emptied, save a few who continued to hold steady the saloon. A parade of bearded men took grip of their hurdy girl and awaited the signal.

Jack slapped Shannon on the arm and said, "Better get to it," and pointed.

Two girls sat in high-backed fuchsia chairs and the men grabbed them and led them to the floor. Shannon said, "My dear, you smell like a summer rose," and indeed she did. The fiddler nodded to the piano player, who tickled a varsovienne on a battered upright wheeled in from Tucson from before the rails came through. The men spun and danced and twirled with exuberance as if unaware of the music's mood or cadence. The women giggled and held on for dear life. The girl wrapped her forearms around Jack's neck tight as he spun her. The bartender signaled to the fiddler, who increased the step of the tune. Jack twirled her while circling, hat overhead, and hooting and snorting like a beast from the hills released upon town.

The music stopped suddenly. Men and women alike fell to the floor, short of breath, and inhaling laughs. Shannon grabbed the hand of the young girl and helped her to her feet. She brushed off her dress, curtsied and said, "Such a gentleman."

The girls led them back to the table and they fell into their chairs. A waiter girl balancing a tray stepped to the table. She served two whiskeys and as many glasses of a clear liquid for the ladies. All drank. Before anything could be said to Shannon's hurdy girl, a large cowboy came over and removed her from the table. She did not look back. Jack said to his girl, "Where is ye friend going?"

"That one? Sure is popular with the cowpokes."

"I can certainly see why."

She said, "Hey, now what about me?"

"Oh now, ye as gorgeous as the new morning sunrise."

"You're just saying that."

"I ain't. I mean it as the day is long."

"Well, then take me to the bar and buy me another drink. Sure am thirsty." She placed her hand on her cheek.

"All right. Shannon, I am fixing on buying her a drink."

Shannon waved his cigarette in the air. "Go. Go. Off with you!"

The second fiddler was sitting on the stage in front of the upright. With the lead and the piano player fetching whiskey, he spoke to a tall hurdy girl. Her dress a soft yellow, unstained, and flowing freely above the soot-covered floor. Her right hand rested on the fiddler's shoulder and she laughed, filling the space above the muddled speech of the patrons. She ran her fingers down the fiddler's cheek and he looked down and blushed. She turned and her dark hair waved over her shoulder and she stood at a stare, directly at Shannon. They locked eyes. She smiled, as did he. She slowly put one foot in front of the other and stood before him at the table. "Well," she said. Shannon stood and pushed back the chair for her as she sat. It was then he noticed her left arm was missing.

A stub of a thing, which came to a point of sorts, and at the tip, something of a belly button. Shannon tipped his hat. "What a gentleman," she said. "Are you usually this rude to a lady?"

"How do you mean, miss?"

"I'm sitting here without drink for more than a few seconds now."

Shannon grinned, "How do you propose we fix that?"

"I'll be damned. A man asking a woman for advice."

She looked back and fixed her hair over her ear and Shannon just stared at her and put his hand under his chin. She whistled and the waiter girl trudged over with the tray and laid down two glasses. She looked up at the girl and said, "The other stuff, May Belle. How many times I tell you, girl?" She grabbed a whiskey off the tray and shooed May Belle off back behind the bar.

Shannon said, "You might be getting in some hot water." Shannon raised his eyebrows and spied May Belle at Screed's side, pointing behind her. Screed shook his head.

She looked over and said, "Could not give less of a damn." They toasted and drank.

"Another, another," she yelled and May Belle approached the table under the eye of Screed, who followed and said, "Bonnie, now what in all hell do you think you're doing?"

"Go to hell, Robert," she said.

Screed shook his head. "I'm through with her, May Belle. I am through with her."

May Belle obliged and Shannon toasted to things past and she toasted to things forgotten and they laughed and drank. The hall had dimmed and a yellow haze became the place. The sweet smell of cherry pipe burned somewhere and the wears of such crept along the ceiling. The fiddler stood.

"Gentlemen, find yourself a partner for the next dance!" Shannon stood and he extended his hand, "Miss, may this dance be ours."

"My what a gentleman. But of course."

Bonnie took his hand and face-to-face they stood. Shannon said, "You smell of fresh morning dew off Clew Bay."

She smiled and rubbed her hand down the back of his neck. "Why, I never," she said. The second fiddler started a schottische, when given the nod by the bartender and as Shannon began to spin, she leaned her head back and began to slip away. May Belle peeked from behind the bar and looked up at Screed. He shook his head.

The lamp wore a soft halo and began to flicker. Hours passed and low grew the whale oil that fueled the flame. Shannon stared at the ceiling and into the cracks and spaces of the wood above him. He ran his finger down her exposed back. Bonnie lay off him, with her half arm over his chest. She giggled when his hand drew along her spine, under her hair, and around her neck. Shannon said, "What fate brought us to this moment?" He scratched the dry skin around the socket of her nub and she smiled and told.

"I came by way of Colorado. Sometime after the big freeze. Daddy was hired to drive a supply wagon to a ranch outside Pueblo and never turned back. He didn't think much of them hunting him on account of a mule and wagon. He took me on to Leadville to try his hand at mining. Hard winters. Hard winters." She lifted her chin and placed it on his chest. "There he died of consumption. He was a hard man. Drank most nights and beat on me when he did. No coffin could be afforded. He only left a gambling debt at the saloon and a collection of empty whiskey bottles. I watched the undertaker wrap his body in burlap and they lowered him into a frozen hole. A plank laid over him. Weighted on by rocks to fend off wolves.

"Our neighbor, a kind man he was, put in my hand a small sack. Inside a pinch or two of gold dust in exchange for my father's whiskey bottles. The empty bottles. I still remember him leaving the cabin with them bottles. He stopped. Stopped in the door. Looked back at me. He turned and walked into the snow and I could hear his boots making tracks. I still remember that. I just sat in that cabin for weeks. Came up with buying a ticket to La Junta. I got there and in that station. I just sat. Just sat. I was supposed to be moving on to Texas but I knew there wasn't nothing calling me there. I just got up and switched tracks. Went south and ended up in Benson. And here I am lying on you in Willcox." She did not mention her arm. He touched it and she looked up through her dark. He did not ask. She did not further tell.

Shannon rolled on his side and reached over her grabbing a thin cigar from a stand where an ashtray and bottle sat. She produced a match and he puffed sending the smoke rising to the stained ceiling. Bonnie ran her painted nails down his back and she watched her hand in the black reflection of the window. He puffed again and blew the smoke out of the corner of his mouth.

Shannon said, "The first thing. My first memory. A young lad. In Saint Patrick's and there in the pew I was in amazement of the Jesus and the clouds. The light above through the colored panes. My hands were folded and I looked over at my mother. She was rocking there in the pew holding her rosary. Uttering the prayers to herself. In silence. The silence of that church with Jesus there bursting through the clouds. We left church, you see. Mother was holding my hand. Walking down camp. We passed the square and there a patch of these yellow flowers. They were the finest yellow I'd seen. I asked Mother if she knew what kind of flowers they be. She could not recall the name. I asked permission to smell them. I walked over and bent down to smell. There in the flower was a dead bee. Curled up like a babe. There dead. I just froze and gazed into this flower cradling the dead bee. Mother came over and hurried me off. Aye. Well, I don't know why but that is my first memory. My father had passed by this time. That I am sure of at least because I cannot recall him." Shannon sat up against the bed board and Bonnie lay on his lap, looking up at him still. He ran his hand through her hair.

"Whiskey, whiskey," she said. Shannon tipped the bottle into her mouth and it dripped out of the creases of her lips. She coughed.

Shannon said, "Careful now," and continued. "Mother had a small picture of him. Brittle little thing from a few days after they landed in New Orleans. They caught a freighter from Liverpool. Paid the way in the kitchen or so she told me. To the canal he went, like so many. There he lies still to this day. In some levee or ditch like the many of them. It's lined with the bodies of the Irish like torches leading the way. The canal might as well be one of blood." Shannon had the cigar between his fingers, his skin brown where flesh pressed on leaf. He puffed and ran his hand across her left shoulder.

"Mother. She kept quarters for a banker at Hibernian. Proud she was. Proud. Often I would come play with their children. Running in the short grass of the garden and throwing the ball. Round that time she met a man. My stepfather. I hesitate to call him such a title. As he did not live up to even such a low calling." Shannon took a deep chug from the bottle. "She married him. She did. He was a man from the bank. A teller. I later heard he was the man who wore a tie and a flower on his lapel. Always a flower. She didn't have the heart to tell me, you know? Instead the father did one day after Sunday service. He pulled me aside and talked to me. 'Son,' he said. He started with 'son.' He informed me, the good man, of my mother's marriage. Over his shoulder. Jesus in the clouds. Bursting over his shoulder. After he was through he patted my shoulder and said, 'God be with you,' and that was it. I walked out onto camp and there he was with my mother, holding her hand. She never spoke about it. Nor did I. Not even the day he left her.

"Not long after that day at church. On to Houston. Hugh was his name. Hugh Walterson. The half-English snake had saved his pennies and had sights on being the proprietor of a mercantile. See now, he knew how much money Mother had. He was the teller, see? The bastard. On the train to Houston. First time I laid foot on the iron horse. I felt the beating of rails in my bones. When we pulled out of Union Station and crossed over the Mississippi, which was the farthest I'd been from home. I remember the cypress hung with mosslike drapes on those green lowlands. I knew right then I would never set my eyes on the city again and I was not wrong. Houston came and along with it the store. Mother tended the counter and he stocked and did any number of things. Included in that, a healthy whiskey habit. He made quite an order of it. Drinking the profit and coming down on me often. It was then I went to the rails. A boy from the corner would spin me yarns about adventure. I took the bait and was off. Caught my first freighter and spent the next number of years tramping around Texas on the Santa Fe. The Katy. Fort Worth, Dallas, Weatherford for a time.

"I would come back often. Mother would eventually stop yelling about the danger of riding but Hugh kept drinking. I would notice bruises and one time a decent shiner on her. Where is that whiskey?" Shannon grabbed the bottle and poured it gently into Bonnie's mouth and then lifted it onto his. "Oh, I fought the snake. Fought him well I did. Got the best of him a few times. But never did last. He was bigger. A bigger bastard than I. One time, I caught the Katy and tramped up

94

to Waco and just turned back from there. Got back and the store was closed. Shelves empty. It had only been a week. He sold all the stock and took up with some young whore and went on to Tulsa, I later discovered. I inquired at his haunts. Finally, in a saloon he slimed the floors in, I found the clue. Cattle. A drunk said cattle. He bought into cattle.

"Some friends pulled money together for Mother. I worked the harvest to give her enough to settle down somewhere. On to Galveston she went. She took up house work again and after time was pleased to look out on the ocean. Walk the sand. Collect flotsam and shells. She had a small house a throw from the sea. That's how I left her. I'm glad that's how I remember her. I went on to San Antonio. Some newsboy yells out about the storm and I knew then she was gone. I grabbed the paper from him and ran. Young lad could not keep up and gave way after a block or two. I cried over that damn paper. I used my last dollar to get blind drunk. I then crawled out of the bar and into a sewer.

"Went on to the station and just walked along the tracks till I hit a jungle and fell. Don't know how long I lay there but I looked up and some bum was just staring at me. I sat up and pointed." Shannon raised his arm, whiskey bottle in hand. "I pointed. I said, what is that way? And out of his dirty grime of a face, his hole uttered, 'The west.' That's what he said. The next train I hopped was headed west. There's a purpose to all this." Shannon sucked on the bottle. "God has his ways and I'll have my day." Bonnie took the cigar and blew smoke onto the ceiling. The lamp puttered to a low and shadows crept on the walls. The room slowly went dark.

The sound of an empty bottle hitting the floor roused him from sleep. Shannon shook and covered his eyes when the sun struck him through a break in the curtains. Jack leaned against the door with his shirt bunched in his hand and said, "Morning." Shannon felt the sheets and peered over the side of the bed. "Where is she?"

Jack said, "She?"

"Bonnie. Was she here when you came in?"

"Nope. You was by ye lonesome. Who's she?"

Shannon threw his legs over the side of the bed. Dew shook down the window as a cart cobbled past, the driver yelling at human traffic to give way. Shannon reached down and covered himself with his shirt. He buttoned it and said, "A gentleman never tells."

Jack said, "You expecting me to take ye for one?"

Shannon stood and put on his paints and lifted the mattress. He removed his tattered billfold, examined the contents and shoved it in his back pocket. He said, "A real sweetheart. A jewel."

Jack buttoned his shirt. "Any bed that ain't crawling with centipede and spiders is a sweetheart to me. How much money we got left?"

Shannon slapped Jack on the back as he walked past. "Enough for a fine breakfast."

They plodded down the stairs and a short, skinny clerk at the desk watched them over his glasses. When they reached the bottom, he put down his newspaper and removed the spectacles, rolling them between his fingers. "Morning, gentleman," he said. "Trust you had a comfortable sleep?"

Jack said, "Did indeed. Now looking for a hearty breakfast."

"Of course," the clerk said. "Step back into the hall and you will find most all you desire this morning."

Jack tipped his hat and followed Shannon through the doorframe and stepped down into the hall. Jack said, "Sure looks different."

"Aye. Whiskey and women will change the decor of most places."

The tables now covered in white cloth and blue, fancy trim, glass could be heard clinking from a back room and the rough oval tables hosted men in open jackets and suits and derby hats hung in all directions. One with top hat, puffing a cigar and waving to the waiter, called for more coffee. A spotted napkin hung from his collar. He looked at Shannon and Jack as they sat, shook his newspaper and went on to reading.

A boy came from the kitchen with a silver pot and filled up his cup and moved on. "Coffee?"

"Yes, sir," said Jack.

Shannon said, "Bring on the waiter, son," as he drew a match and lit a cigarette.

"I can take ye order," the boy said.

Shannon said, "Have you oysters?"

"Yes, sir."

"Have you eggs?"

"Yes, sir. We got eggs too."

"Have you celery?"

"Yes, sir. I believe we do."

"Oysters, eggs, celery and some bread, son."

"Yes, sir."

"Oh, and pour the coffee, lad."

The boy poured.

The man shook his paper and turned the page.

Jack squinted at the man and fixed a napkin in his lap. "Boy," he said. "What's he eatin'?"

The boy jerked his head. "Him?"

Jack nodded.

"Creamed duck and peas."

Shannon said, "You want duck?"

"Nah, had me enough of duck in Texas once. Ain't had it since. Well. Let me correct that. They was geese. Not duck. Was outside of Big Spring riding from Abilene. Come on this water and just about as far man could see. Geese. As many stars in the sky was geese on that water. Just honking away. Not a care in the bird world. I just sat and picked them off. The ones close to the shore that is. Just waded out and gathered them. Roasted them up real quick. There was a wind and I was plucking and they would just ride the breeze. Some fool downwind would swear it was snowing. Good eating, just too damn much. I smoked some and it kept me riding through Odessa and almost on to El Paso, if you can believe that. Then I picked off gopher but them geese spoiled me. Haven't touched waterfowl since."

"And when was that?"

Jack leaned back in his chair and ran his finger between his cheek and teeth. "Seventy-nine, I reckon. Just about another lifetime ago." Jack spat on the floor. "Shoulda kept on riding. Shoulda kept on riding. Almost did. I recall riding out of El Paso on the Fourth of July of all days and stopping the horse on top of this ridge. Just past sunrise and almost as hot as noon it was. There was a mist along the scrub below. I could see for miles. There was these dark birds circling above me. A whole mess of them. I figured them vultures but as I watched they began to dip. They was eagles. All of them.

Eagles and these low clouds stretching forever. The sun hit those clouds and a mist of gold and blue rose. And ain't never seen the ocean but thought it must look like this. Rode down into it and I thought I'd just keep riding. I made up my mind there. I'd ride to the ocean and figure it out when I sat there in front of it. Where to go then? I learned enough on the trail. Certain as one of the last damn fools to travel down it the wrong way. Hell. Should a kept on riding."

"And what the hell stopped you, Jack?"

Jack leaned back into his chair and patted his pockets. "Damn, must've misplaced the cigarettes. Could you oblige?"

"Aye."

"Match?" Shannon cut a match on the table and lit Jack's cigarette. "What stopped me? There are only two circumstances that will stop a man from his destiny." Shannon lifted his eyebrows and grinned. The cigarette in between his fingers turned smoke over his face. "Ye waiting for it ain't you? I'll tell ye. War, whiskey and women."

"Now, Jack, that's three."

"That's three ain't it? I stand corrected. There are three circumstances that will stop a man from his destiny. From there on he is resounded to his fate. Fate ain't pretty. You know what it feels like?"

"Fate? No, but I have a sense you are about to explain it to me."

"You listening now? Like a fat grain of sand in ye eye. Ever have a fat grain of sand in ye eye?"

"No, Jack. Can't say I have."

Jack propped in his chair. "I'll tell you, friend. When you have it. You will know it."

Shannon twisted the cigarette out on the floor. "Will that be fate then?"

Jack shrugged. "If it is. Ye find out soon enough."

The man shook his paper and huffed. "Boy!" he shouted. "Waiter! The bill. The bill. Cannot miss this train, son!"

The boy came carrying the oysters. Two dozen or so open and piled together. "Be right back with the eggs and celery," the boy said.

"Boy!" the man yelled.

Jack shook his head. "Some bastard that one is."

Shannon slurped on the shell and leaned over the table with juice running off his chin. "Real one, that."

The boy returned and placed the eggs and celery on the table. The man in top hat looked over his bill and fiddled with his wallet. He gathered his things and passed.

Jack said, "Howdy."

The man stopped and spun his head. His face bunched and red. "Yes?"

"Where you headed?"

"As if it was any business of yours, sir."

"Mister, you need to learn some manners I'd offer."

The man huffed. "You, sir, have not been asked to offer."

"Better git," Jack said. "That whistle bound to blow."

The man stomped off through the door and out of the lobby, where the short, skinny clerk folded his newspaper and watched him leave over his spectacles.

Shannon said, "Sure made his day, Jack. Now enjoy your breakfast."

Jack bent over his plate. "I'm fixing to now."

The boy stood at the end of the bar. Jack nodded to him. Out of the kitchen the boy brought a steaming pot of fresh. "More coffee, sir?"

After breakfast they walked Railroad Avenue. They dipped into a store on the corner of Stewart and came out wearing a firsthand change of clothes and more than a few penny cigars. Shannon handed two cigars to Jack and they kept a slow stroll toward the station. Putting their backs to the posts of the Willcox Hotel, they smoked and watched the comings and goings of people and freight. Cattle cars stretched the length of the town. The low calls of the beeves could be heard as a constant hum. The heat began to give way to the stench of manure. The sweetness of the cigars kept the spectators from fleeing the smell. Jack knelt and spat. A round man with a three-piece suit and a large head asked Jack if this was the hotel where one of the Earp boys had met his end. Jack looked at Shannon and they both shrugged. Jack said, "Sorry, can't say I know the poor bastard." The man tipped his hat and Jack in turn. The man moved on. Mules carrying cords of knotted firewood passed, kicking up the packed sand. A Mexican followed carrying a pail of water and talking to the mules.

When the path of the sun reached close to noon, Shannon nudged Jack, who was drifting off and said, "Let's go."

Back to the Buffalo Saloon. Both leaned into the bar and looked into the mirror. Each could not believe the same two stood in the very spot, just the evening before, ragged and filthy. The barman did not seem to make them. Jack called for two beers and they drank with speed and great thirst. Two more followed along with a toast to the Republic. An old, bearded man at the end of the bar stood and slammed his cane on the floor. Jack laughed and Shannon told him to keep his nerve. The barman spoke to the old man and he nodded his head and stared at Jack. Shannon bought the man a drink and after the old man finished such, he limped out of the saloon. The barman said, "Some is still fighting the war," and he served up a free lunch of beef in thick brown sauce.

Shannon said, "When does the faro table come on?"

The barman said, "Shortly. Perhaps an hour or two."

Jack shook his head. "Why?"

"Lady Luck. Lady Luck."

"How much money ye got left?"

"Ten dollars. Could double it again."

"Suit yourself," Jack said. "Just don't lose it all."

Shannon pushed the back of his hat up.

They passed the hours trading places at the bar and the slopes and toasting and buying cigars. They ventured outside on occasion and watched the shadow of the wind turbine grow skinny over the sunbaked avenue. Trains kept a steady pace of departure, followed by the arrival of cowhands and ranchers coming to the west side to spree in the gurdy houses and saloons. Before long the bar was steaming with the men of the range and rails. The room took on an oily manure smell with wafting cigars and shouts of reverie. Games of chance materialized. The bank holder set up and called for the next lucky man to step forward. Shannon offered that was him. Jack slurred, "Don't lose all the damn money." Jack closed his eyes and his head slung to the side and he thought he may have drank too much.

Shannon smacked Jack awake. "Let's go," he said.

Shannon walked out and sat on the step. The glow of sunset hung orange to the west and with it a blue haze began to creep from the east. Jack grabbed Shannon's shoulder and steadied himself to a seat. "Hell," he said. "I was just starting to take a fancy to that place. What's the name of it anyhow?" He looked around expecting someone to answer. Shannon spat and wiped his mouth with his open palm and studied it.

"Shannon, tell me you just didn't blow it all."

"No, I was smart enough not to do that. But dumb enough not to get as sauced as you are now."

Jack fanned away invisible pets. "This stop is only half a decent cow town. How much we got left anyhow?"

"One dollar. One damn dollar."

Jack threw his hat up and caught it. "One dollar can git ye nice 'n red in this country. How about it?"

Shannon pulled his fingers over his mouth. "The rings. The rings is left."

The hat was back on Jack's head. "Don't tell me ye holdin' them?"

Shannon shook his head. "I'm no fool."

"What do you aim to do with them then?"

"I hawk them now or never the way I see it."

From out of the saloon, a man stumbled between them and fell face forward into the dirt and he did not move afterward. Horses tied and watering whimpered and became nervous.

Jack said, "Best move on from this spot."

They stopped at a slim and leafless tree whose branches stretched like impoverished fingers. Shannon handed Jack twenty-five cents and told him to wait for him back at the saloon.

"I'll find a deal on the rings somewhere on this west side. If I don't come back."

Jack waved his hand. "If you don't come back? Hell, boy. Just get ye ass back here." He stood swaying and watched Shannon dissolve into the night.

Jack floated through the gathering crowds of hollering cowboys congregating between saloons and halls to trade barbs and slaps on the back, every man armed and drinking and none paying close attention to the bearded drunk who appeared without holster. Two cowboys helped Jack into the saloon. He was then wedged between bar, wall, and a large spittoon, then helped with drink. They had large hats and wore pointed mustaches and red bandanas. They paid in small coin and prescribed a whiskey for him. The barman agreed. He drifted and thought at one point he may have fell or taken for sleep. A man took position next to him and put a bitter liquid, that he thought may have been coffee, to his lips.

Jack opened his eyes and breathed deeply. The man pounded on his back and asked if he was feeling it. Jack said, "What the hell might be it?" His eyes watered and nose ran. The cheap fiddle music spun high in his skull.

The man wiped Jack's face with a greasy rag from off the bar. He gave him a stool and Jack sat, breathing deeply. The man stood facing him with his elbow on the bar. "Never has not worked," the man said.

Jack stood and placed his hands on his knees. The floor bubbled with vomit. "When did all that happen?"

The man said, "Just a few minutes ago. It took a bit for you to come to."

Jack inched over to the steel bar along the wall and grabbed hold and heaved and spat in the spittoon. "Don't pay it much mind, mister. There been worse things on that floor. Seen it myself. Don't care to tell it though." Jack looked up at the voice. He was young and with pale eyes. His cheeks sunk with the makings of a beard. His jacket was an unusual green, on which he wore a flower. He tipped his short-brimmed hat when he saw Jack's eyes.

The man said, "Pleased, I'm sure. Charles Busenbark is what my father named me."

Straitening himself, Jack stretched out his balmy hand and Charles shook it firm and straight. "I take it you had a hell of a night so far."

Jack said, "Any damn water in this hole?"

Charles called for water and the barman brought over a stein with dragon handle. Jack spilled the stein over his mouth and in the occurrence managed to down some. Jack slammed the stein down and Charles said, "Looks like ye ready for another whiskey." Charles toasted to the health of his new friend. "And what they call you?"

"Jack."

"To Jack's constitution!"

They drank and the barman looked over his shoulder and joined them.

"Where you from, Jack?"

"Charles, when folk ask me I generally say Shakespeare."

"Hell," said Charles. "You're generally from a place that don't exist no more?"

Jack said, "You would be correct on that point. But I aim to change that somehow. Rough in these parts?"

"You got no idea, Jack."

Removing his hat Jack placed it over the stein and wiped his forehead with his sleeve. "Now you want to tell me what the hell you fed me?"

Charles grinned. "Oh now, Jack, it's a secret but ain't too much of one. Just an old Indian tonic."

Jack squinted. "And you just had it on ye?"

"Matter of fact. I did. Just came in from the trail. Gone thirty days from San Carlos. My father trades with Apache up there. We bullwhack it up there on the supply routes. Normally I just beat it home, which is on the other side of the tracks. Last two days, God been smiling down on us. Clear weather and clearer trail. Ole Joe went to tend to the shed, so I came round for a pick me up before heading back."

Jack shook his head. "And where do I come in?"

"Damn near tripped over you on the way to the bar. Like a sack of rocks lying on the floor. I asked Tobiath here the story and all he said was, you was drunk. I had me a full bottle of the tonic in the wagon. Here I am. Here you are. Back to ye feet."

"A debt of gratitude is owed to you then, Charles." Jack searched his jacket and turned out his pockets. "I know I had some on me. Must have dropped it or one of them cowboys who helped me, helped themselves to it. I'd go a round with you but ye have to forgive me."

Charles looked around and smiled. "Jack, I promise this. I am here standing next to the best company in this here saloon. Wouldn't have it any other way, friend. In fact. Next round on me. Tobiath! Send another two down along with something fizzy to wash it all down."

Tobiath was a large man with sideburns like moss above a finely trimmed beard. His stature won in the mines pushing carts and he took his trade elsewhere, with only a stout fool to cross him. He served up whiskey and beer and again joined up on the libations. Again a toast to Jack's health, who started to regain his color, with sweat beginning to abide.

Jack told him of his journey west and of the silver mines of Shakespeare. Charles told of the Apache medicine men and the dances witnessed in San Carlos at sunrise. Painted bodies and headdresses lined with dark feathers and of cries to the earth or some God unknown to him. He told of trading with chiefs and councils and of renegades that would ride to meet them early on the trail. Charles raised the grimy tonic to the light and shook it. Grinds of matter clung to the sides of the glass and slid back into the concoction. Charles said, "Yes, sir. This one will bring you back from the edge. Others will take you there." Charles slipped the vial back into his pocket and took a last gulp of his beer. Jack listened and drank over the incessant whine of the fiddle and pitched sing-alongs to old ballads and archaic hill songs.

The moon was full against the night sky and hung with a halo there, tacked to the dark wall of the universe. Stepping out on the avenue, Charles shooed off a big hat, heavy in drink, leaning half asleep on his cab. Charles circled and inspected the wagon and the contents of such. Woven blankets and black porous rocks filled crates that lined the inside of the covered wagon. Jack lit one of the cigars he found in the inside pocket of his coat and passed the other to Charles, as he stepped into the coach and took hold of the reins. Looking down at Jack from the perch, he smiled. "Much obliged. Much obliged," he said. "Before we part, old friend. I have a gift for you. Hold on." He turned and reached into a sack behind him and produced a small pouch. Plain in the color of terra, it bore no markings, but a single red bead dangling from the bottom.

Jack studied it and looked up at Charles. "Thank ye. What the hell is it?"

Charles placed the cigar between his fingers and blew out. "Jack, like I told you before. Some take you back from the edge. Some bring you there."

Jack said, "I am guessing I have to trust you on that one."

Charles tipped his hat and said, "Your journey will bring you there." Jack took hold of the harness and led the horse around and waved to Charles as the cart rattled away from his spot under the crown of the moon.

Jack bowed and there stood Shannon, hands deep in the pockets of his coat and collar up. Jack said, "You see. I knew you'd be back."

Shannon shrugged. "Aye." The brim of his hat pointing heaven and shadow falling upon his eyes. "Did you manage to have any fun without me?"

"Not much to speak of and you might not even believe it."

Shannon looked down at Jack's hand. "And what do you have there then?"

Jack squeezed the pouch. "Not entirely sure about that one. A gift from a friend."

"Gifts are precious things in this here world," said Shannon.

"As are friends. You move them rings?"

"Sold them off to a Mexican. He overpaid. I suppose he wanted them to melt down. But I did not inquire nor did he offer." Jack looked up at the stars and he strained to understand them over the dangling lamp lights of the facades. Jack said, "And where to now?" Shannon looked down the avenue.

"You fellas gonna come in?"

Shannon peered through the window and into the hall, staring at her through the foggy window.

"Never intended to be a peephole. Hey, fella? You gonna come in?" The doorman with rough brown coat and curled cattle hat poked him. "Come on now."

Shannon juddered and stepped forward. "Mind your business, lad. I'm a guest at this establishment."

The man stepped back. "Fine. Fine. That fact will be determined." He stepped inside. Shannon hunched over and directed his eye back inside. And there she spun. Head back and tilted. She bore a collar of black ribbon, the same flowing dress, hat with bird and lace and on this night, she was a red-head. She laughed along with a clean fellow in tan suit, much like the color of the wilderness beyond. The doorman stepped out of the entrance to the hotel with the skinny clerk, who removed his glasses and studied him. The clerk nodded.

Shannon said, "Lad, come here."

The skinny clerk said, "I think he all means you, Lionel."

Lionel bobbed and fixed his belt buckle. "What is it?"

Shannon waved for him to come closer and he did. "Open the door a crack."

Lionel did such and Shannon said, "Now, see that girl. The one in hat and lace?"

Lionel said, "You kidding me? There must be ten of them in hat and lace."

"Fine," Shannon said. "The skinny one with the bird on her hat."

"Bird on her hat?"

"The one with one arm."

"Oh, Rose you mean?"

"Is that her name?"

"Yes, I do believe it is."

Jack leaned back against the hitch and smoked. He had no words. He just smoked. Shannon raised his chin and edged the corners of his mouth southward. Jack threw down his cigarette.

Shannon said, "One more thing. Lionel, is it?"

"Yes. That's my Christian name."

Shannon stepped toward him. "Would you happen to know if she has ever been in Colorado?"

Lionel scratched his chin. "Damned if I know. So many of them, you see? You ain't sweet on her is ye? Last fella got ran outta town by Screed. Busted him up real good."

The lobby was empty again save for the skinny clerk in glasses peering over his newspaper. The desk he supported himself on was much like one of a schoolteacher, with raised stool to match. Shannon ignored him and hovered by the passage to the hall, where he stood nodding his head to the music. He stared off beyond the dancers, in some trance state. A jumble of song and shrill laughing filled the corners of the lobby. Jack stopped and waited for Shannon. The skinny clerk said, "Tell you what, friend. A man might think the world has gone to hell picking up one of these."

Jack said, "What would that be?"

The man shook the paper. "Why the newspaper. It's either roses or manure." He stuck his nose close to the page. "This here. Listen. Everly Baker joined the Woman's League just on Saturday. How do you like that? Don't ask me what they do with their time. I bet a nickel it's not far from what those Masons do behind closed doors. Hoods and swords and well it's terrible to think. God help us. Then, this in the next item. A Black feller burned at the stake in Colorado. Can you believe that one? I kid you not." His mustache glistened with saliva, hanging just above his top lip. He shook the paper. "Now I know this country here seen some of its own sour times but. Burned at the stake? Can't say I know what to think about this world. Jesus gonna be here." He shook his head and continued.

"But don't think that's it. No. Do not think it. Item here from these parts. Like I said this country here has its own set of indigents that bless us with their presence every season. Just east. Poor man. Body found buried in a pile of ore it says here. Lost his life not long ago. Let me see. Says here the blood began to seep from the rock. The ore turned it black. They thought the old boy took for the hills again, being an old-timer and all. But a black puddle oozed from the rock and someone finally had the good sense to take a shovel and put their back into it. Stabbed, he was. In the neck, says here. Yes, sir, and it don't take a railroad detective not a day on the job to know the breed of traveler they seek. No, sir. The fiend lucked out, as the poor man just collected wages for the week. Fool took his rings too says here." He folded the paper in half and placed it upright on the desk. "Enough tramps come through here. A menace. And those are just the ones begging at the back doors. This breed here is ready to kill you for a nickel, friend." He shook his head. His face strained with the confusion of a brooding puzzle. "Watch yourself."

Jack's eyes betrayed nothing to the skinny clerk. His palms were still flat on the desk and he tucked them into his jacket pockets and said, "I always have one eye elsewhere. Keeps me out of trouble with the gents and in trouble with the ladies." The skinny clerk stared at him and unfolded his paper and resumed his quiet and horrible study of worldly events. Jack stepped back and tipped his hat. The man did not acknowledge the gesture. Shannon still swayed and spied on the swirling inside the hall. There Bonnie, or Rose, sat with whiskey in hand, entertaining a bearded man in large hat. She removed it and fanned his face with the wide brim. They laughed. Jack spun Shannon around with a hand on his shoulder. Jack said, "What did you aim to do tonight?" Shannon stared back at him. "In that case. Come on. Let's get on up to one of them rooms." The skinny clerk peered over the paper and watched as they climbed the staircase.

Shannon looked down on the scene in front of the hotel. With the early hours approaching, foot traffic had begun to die down. The music from the hall held a faint presence in the air and the thump of the cadence was muffled through the thick wood. Jack sat on the bed and said, "Only took them a day or so to find that poor man."

"Keep your voice down," he whispered back at Jack. "So, they found it. Bound to happen sooner or later."

Jack said, "Later would have been kinder for our sake. Yours more so."

Shannon said, "They would hang us both."

"I reckon, but damn sure you'll be first."

Shannon removed his jacket and threw it onto the stiff chair in the corner. He unbuttoned his vest and grabbed the whiskey bottle.

Jack said, "Something wrong with your eyes too?"

Shannon placed the empty bottle down on the desk.

Shannon said, "Wishful thinking."

Jack lay back on the bed. "What do you aim to do?"

Shannon ran his fingers over his face. "Get drunk."

"And then?"

"We set off at dawn."

Jack nodded. "How much from the rings we got left?"

Shannon patted his vest pocket. "Certainly enough."

"Enough to pay on to the next stop?"

Shannon laughed. "Pay a fare to ride a train? You are joking?"

Jack sat up. "The body was on the west side of the track. The dicks will be eyeing the stations and camps for tramps going west. You reckon a posse ain't been formed? None will suspect paying customers out of this hole. I'm not going down here, in this desert and from where I sit." Jack patted the bed. "You owe me one. We ride the cushions on to Benson."

Shannon pursed his lips. "Aye. Aye."

Jack nodded. "Alright then, there some unfinished business still."

"Oh?"

"Who's the fool gonna run down and fetch a bottle of the stuff?"

5: BENSON

Jack rubbed his eyes and stared out the vibrating window. Before him a vast dry lake shimmered into a horizon of rock. Wind ripped the far reaches of this body and Jack pointed out to the heat flowing over the surface, rising in waves. Shannon sat with fist under chin. Eyes strained. The iridescent lights pulsed between white birds feeding on algae and salt grass. A wall of clouds stretched before the black giants in the far wilderness and the white formations reflected off the glass surface. At the center, a diamond shining, like the beating heart of this place. Jack's eyes watered and he pulled a handkerchief out of Shannon's breast pocket. Shannon said, "Don't tell me you're crying?"

"Me? Hell, no. Been staring out so long my vision's blurring."

The train rolled on and the lake grew brown and receded toward the hills, until tiny black islands dotted the horizon and shrunk into the solar bed of cracked desert. Jack could not recall a time he felt as clean as his person did now. The water in the hotel's tin basin may well have been oil when he dripped out of the murky water. Years of trail dust and grime settled at the bottom and would later clog when the attendant went on to drain it. A scissor to his beard and the fresh cotton and canvas he wore gave him an air of society, however faint the sensation, as they stood at the station with citizenry. There Jack nudged Shannon to the ticket window where he paid for coach. Shannon did not hesitate to claim the fare the first paid since he had ridden across the Mississippi as a boy. He swore it would be his last. Jack answered by holding a cigar aloft and producing a match, his thoughts written in the smoke. He rubbed the ash into the crimson cushion and slouched into the window. Shannon began to feel the past two evenings and the throb of the tracks slowly coaxed his lids to succumb to their request.

Jack woke as the train slowed and out the window a small white station passed. Children and a man in straw hat with donkey stood idle, awaiting the cars to pass. Jack opened his eyes again and looked over to Shannon, whose hat was well over his brow, his head back against the seat. Out on the plain stood buttes and an axis of crags born of limestone and shaped from the will of wind and rain eons old. Jack drifted and awoke when a baby's cry marked the rail meeting a grade and then began the climb through the pass of the Dragoons. There was little movement in the car despite the number of passengers. A man to his right paged through a Bible and stuck his head out in the aisle to investigate the child's wail.

The sun outlined folds in the mountains, which ran dark and slopped into ancient coarse granite. A flat cloud sat over distant and hidden peaks. The only movement detectable there was shadows lapping over back reaches of the range and creeping slowly over crags. Hoodoos stood in this country. Here they stood whittled as witnesses to this cosmic wilderness and bear on their surface the time of this land. The train did slow again and the conductor emerged in blue suit and tilted cap and called out, "Dragoon." The man with Bible rose and fiddled with his handkerchief. He gathered a bag and walked down the aisle. A tall man in a yellow suit engaged the conductor on the platform. The conductor shook his head and waved at the engineer. No passengers appeared to board and as the train inched out of the station, the yellow suit signaled and inspected the passing faces. Shannon's hat shifted forward with no whistles or machine cry to wake him.

Before long the journey took them into a valley, leading down switchbacks dressed in paloverde and looping through a wide trench. A cathedral of peaks dressed a crown across the sky. Clouds dripped down a far canyon and Jack thought that could mean rain. The country revealed red clay and badlands descending into heavy brush, spotted by saguaro, tall and rooted in sand deposits. Crossing the river, a green bed lay on the sides running each direction toward the rift. Jack rose in his seat, as did the others and looked down into the dark milky run of the watercourse. A woman in front of the car gasped and then all sat. The conductor in blue came around and cried, "Benson."

Jack grabbed the bend of his hat and nudged Shannon with his right elbow. He raised his head and then sat up swiftly. Shannon rubbed his eyes and said, "Miss anything?"

Jack shook his head. "We're here."

The platform stretched the length of the train with two levels for passengers and cargo to gather. The movement of the crowd led to a staircase and a short walk found them on Fourth Street. A wind wafting down off the Rincon had cooled the valley. Men loitered out under the awnings of saloons, all free of coats and outerwear, save their vests and scarves. There was laughter there, with one holding his boot above his head and singing. Three dogs followed the boot, panting and barking. Carriages choked this stretch of thoroughfare with hack drivers calling out gruffly and the sound of hooves drowning the rails and the racket about them. Jack leaned up against a short fence post where others gathered and he lifted back his hat studying the scene. Shannon looked both ways down Fourth Street and looked back at Jack. "Suppose you're hungry?"

Jack said, "Suppose ye right."

Shannon again looked both ways.

Jack said, "Which way you reckon we gonna walk?"

"Hell if I know. Suppose." Shannon pointed to the right of the depot and they walked slowly, as men do with nowhere to go. Others held this pace with them, as some seemed asleep or drunk even at this hour of the early afternoon. Others shuffled past with sacks flung over shoulder and Chinese men with queues bouncing off their backs hurried by. One holding a shovel and the other a bucket. A mule trailed behind and the bucket man called out in tongue to the animal. There followed ten or twelve others, each with pickax and bearing long shirt with wide-brimmed hat. They chattered and kept to their toil and then faded into traffic. Shannon came up on a tousled miner back on his haunches and he inquired about a meal. The miner did not look up and spat. He nodded his head. "Right before ye," he said.

Jack said, "What have ye?"

Shannon pointed. "There."

Jack said, "Hell, a good a place as any from the looks of it." The miner spat and rocked in his place, muttering something to himself. Jack said, "The hills will do that to a man. Seen it myself. Came too close myself."

The sign read Shines Lunch Counter. The false front had been removed and what stood was a long counter, where the bar of a saloon might have been. There were no chairs and men of all cloth inclined into the structure in all manner of ways and threw down grub. Against the wall opposite this counter was a shelf, as long as the former and on it patrons rested glasses full and empty of small beer and coffee. Linens scattered the floor and a man in white apron gathered them. Jack found a place between a man in buckskin coat and a younger fellow in white suit. The mess could be seen through a framed hole in the wall, where crockery was thrown about and tin plates of food handed through. On the wall a chalk-board scribbled with menu and specials.

Jack squinted. "What's it say?"

Shannon's eyes read down the board and rattled off choices. "Rabbit, beef, bacon, beans, oysters, all with bread. Brown sauce. On special, oyster corn stew. Fresh, it says."

The man in white suit came up from his bowl and said, "You gentlemen have intention to order the soup? I will have to swear on the decency of the soup and the chef behind it," his mustache lined with the special and a single drip of the stuff hung just under his nose. The man continued, "Shine himself sets it before you. In fact the oysters are so fresh, you can close your eyes, gentlemen, and taste the Pacific. I'd raise my right hand here if presented." The man grabbed his handkerchief and ran it along his lip and the line disappeared along with his rag into his jacket pocket.

"That is quite the endorsement." Shine stood before them at the counter. His fingers pressed down on the surface and arched as if two tarantulas ready to strike.

"The man himself," said the white suit and he extended his hand greedily and shook Shine's hand with a grip of conviction often reserved for other occasions. Shine smiled. The teeth on the left side of his mouth were crooked and sweat poured down his greasy forehead, which he patted down with his sleeve. His mustache was like the tail of a squirrel, sporting grey at the ends and his weight was healthy, as a recent immigrant from back east.

"Fellas, welcome to Shine's. What can I serve you on this fine day?"

Jack said, "Shine, pleased to make the acquaintance. Dare I say my friend here and me well, been on a bit of an oyster spree."

Shannon looked over at the white suit, his spoon making progress toward his mouth and he slurped down a hunky bit of oyster and again raised his head to reveal the line of broth above his lip. He grinned and said, "You found your poison, friend." Shine had not moved a bone. His fingers still arched and ready to strike. He put his hands together in a fist of prayer and said, "Two bowls of the special. If satisfaction is not reached, I'll give you a dish of rabbit on the house." Both men agreed and the white suit had a wide smile across his face. Shine disappeared through the door to the mess.

Shannon said, "I damn well better like the stew. I don't fancy rabbit."

"Rabbit?" The white suit said, "Don't eat much rabbit in San Francisco. It would be safe to assume none. Perhaps miners in from the Sierra. But I can assure you, gentlemen, we eat lots of oysters out there by the Golden Gate. Oysters for just about every occasion and that does not preclude breakfast, gentlemen. In fact, it demands it."

Shine emerged from the kitchen with two glasses of beer in tow. "Your drinks," he said and dropped them on the counter.

"Ah, yes, travel brings thirst. Travel brings thirst. Drink up, gentlemen," the man in white said.

Jack put down his glass and said, "I gather ye from Californy?"

His spoon stopped midway to his mouth. "Excuse me? Cali? Ah, yes. California. Yes, sir. I am. San Francisco, California. Born and raised. Right under what is now Telegraph Hill in fact. Yes, sir. Born and raised. In fact, I've never ventured this far east before and I'm afraid that statement will soon become lie. My ticket goes all the way to New Orleans and then on to the capital. Yes, sir." He then squatted slightly and brought the spoon to his mouth. "You'll have to excuse my behavior, gentlemen. Not too much time to talk nor eat." Shannon kept to his beer and curled his lips around the rim and took purposeful sips, inspecting the glass as he went.

Jack said, "All the way to Washington? Quite a trip. Quite a trip indeed. On account of some business I figure?"

The man hummed. "Yes, business. Some very unfortunate business, I'm afraid. I'm a doctor. Dr. Hunter, at your service. And you are?"

"Oh now, excuse me, Doctor, I'm Jack and this here is Shannon." Shannon nodded and looked into his beer.

"The pleasure is mine, Jack. But, yes, unfortunate business. I am a doctor of the mind, Jack, and I'm here accompanying a train full of soldiers who are all rather deranged from the Philippines. The rate is alarming. They are sent from

Manila in droves and transported back to San Francisco. Then on to Washington to be placed in asylum. Yes. Yes. This is my first trip out and I'm told to expect more. The way this war is going by the time I arrive back in San Francisco, there will be a platoon awaiting me. And through this beautiful country of ours these men travel staring out the window, as if into an abyss. Often the nights are filled with terror. Screaming. Shaking. Others drooling all over themselves. Many with wounds. Some still fresh it would seem. The stench. Ah, excuse me. Excuse me. You gentlemen are about to eat."

Jack said, "No. No. Excuse us. Should have just minded my own. Instead I'm here spoiling ye meal."

The doctor wiped his mustache with linen that sat crumbled on the bar. "It is settled then. We'll both be excused. Now, I must be on my way. The train is set to depart on the hour and I have one more errand." The doctor tipped his derby and bid farewell. As he crossed the exit, Shine came holding two steaming bowls. "Now, fellas, who ordered the special?"

Shannon rubbed his nose. "We both did," he said.

Shine smiled. "That was easy. Bon appetit." Shine collected the doctor's bowl, spoon and linen and returned back to the mess, where the bowl could be heard dropping into water. The soup teemed with corn and oysters. A swirl of brine and fat dotted the surface and Shannon held the bowl in his hands, drinking the broth with bits trickling down his chin. Shannon stood belly to the bar and waved down Shine, who collected empty plates at the end of the counter, left by travelers who abandoned them for the whistle.

"Shine. Shine," Shannon said.

Shine dried his hands with the towel hung over his shoulder. "What can I do for you, friend?"

"Another special."

Shannon's second bowl stood empty. His spoon clanged on the bottom and he licked the stubble under his bottom lip. Jack picked his teeth and watched the traffic on the street. Shine said, "You fellas sure did enjoy that special." He approached the counter and untied his smudged apron. Folding it over once, he placed it under the counter and gathered the empties.

Jack said, "Mightily."

"My pleasure, boys. My pleasure."

Shannon turned and placed his elbows up on the counter. The place was empty and clean save them and staff. Shine came around the counter with his derby on and grabbed a red cotton jacket off a hook. Shannon said, "Knocking off for the day?"

"Game will be starting soon. I haven't missed the first pitch all season."

"Game?"

"Bisbee versus Benson. Big game today. Could mean the league in the long run."

Jack ran his fingers around the brim of his hat. "Baseball?"

"Yes, sir. You fellas in town?"

Jack said, "Just passing through."

"Well, if you have time to burn. Come on watch the game. Just take this street all the way down. If you hit the mountains, you've gone too far. Can't miss it. Nice to meet you fellas."

Shine waved and the door swayed behind him ... The cook called from the kitchen. "Sorry. We're closed now." There was nothing to look back upon, his face disappearing back into the mess. The sun cut a square beam across the floor and the cracks there left small rigid shadows running down the length of each. A whistle blew and Jack walked out to the stoop. A train pulled out of the station with an American flag draped out of an open window.

The miner was still across the street when Jack left Shine's. He rocked and spat, staring off into the arching blue of the sky. Down Railroad they stopped next to a cattle car to inspect a dead vulture that had fallen victim to buckshot. A pale child in a burlap dress poked at it with a splintered railroad tie. Jack looked back and there the miner stood. He smacked the side of his leg with his fist and swayed as if entranced by symphony deranged on drink. They walked on, led by yells and cheers, clear in the arid air. Beyond the street lay the desert and the distance manifest in hills. Marking this boundary, a crowd stood, among them women and children standing on white benches. Horses waited, tied to carved stumps and on one, a rider sat chewing dried beef. Between these crowds a diamond, with players crouched and waiting on the strike of the ball.

Spectators of the fairer sex lined the bleachers wearing bonnets, sun hats and holding white umbrellas with yellow trim. Jack shook the desert off his lapels, as the two days fresh began to sour with the travel. "Come on, Bisbee!" a railroad man yelled, cupping his hands at the sides of his mouth.

Jack stepped onto the bench and asked, "Who here is winning?"

"Happy to say Bisbee, three to zip. We usually whip these Benson boys. On a roll we are, after we put a hurt on Tombstone last week. That victory was about due. This, well, the same old story I'm afraid."

Shannon took the corner of the lower row and kicked the dirt. He said, "You work the rails?"

The man broke his stare and looked down at Shannon. "Yes, sir. Caffee is the name. Brakeman on the A and S. A special ran up here today for folks to come see the game. Baseball is taking in the territory. No wonder about that. Now look at that arm on the pitcher." Caffee shook his head and continued. "But don't go telling that to Reverend Stump here."

Caffee leaned over and slapped the shoulder of the reverend, who jumped and said, "Caffee, you should have done as
I suggested and missed the train." Caffee laughed and slapped
the side of his leg. The second basemen looked over and spat.

Caffee said, "Reverend, I have to run a special up here
to Benson one Sunday so folks can catch a sermon of yours.
If you deliver standing at the pulpit as well as planted on a
bleacher. They will come, Reverend. They will come." The reverend leaned back. He appeared to have opened his mouth but
said nothing. Caffee continued, "Speaking of catches, I think
your boys might be expecting some sport here, Reverend."

A batter stood with bat to shoulder and formed his
stance. The pitcher looked toward the outfield and the bare-
handed players paced back. The shortstop adjusted his finger-
less glove. He spat. The pitcher nodded and shook the brim
of his cap and took a deep breath. The batter waited with bat
cocked. Someone yelled, "Take ye time, Shelby."

The pitcher wound and released the ball. Necks and
heads followed. A boy jumped to see. The bat swung and the
batter's torso tightened and the crack seemed to reverber-
ate to the far hide-colored hills. The center fielder ran backward and tripped over an errant rock, left by the son of the
first baseman. The pitcher stood with hands on hips, elbows
sharply folded. At the plate, Bisbee gathered in joy. The batter collected his congratulations as the ball came bouncing
into the catcher. Caffee laughed and thought he might have
hurt his leg slapping it as often as he did. "I only do it when

I laugh," he said. "I do it often. Especially watching these Benson boys play."

Benson met at the mound. A rider dismounted and led the horse around the stands to greet the ladies, who were gathered on a bench down the first baseline. The events in the field of play had caused little excitement among the ladies and they spoke softly and giggled loudly when the rider greeted them. He pulled something from his shirt pocket and they gathered round him for a demonstration. Again they laughed and one of them removed his hat and placed it on her head. The ladies cheered. "Go on, Lottie," they called. She took hold of the horn and with the dexterity of a charro stepped into the stirrup and onto the rider's horse. It is not known what caused the horse to catch a fright. It was later presumed to be either the swish of Lottie's skirt or the shrill claps of esteem from the ladies, but the horse took off toward the wilderness, a hair off second base. The center and left fielder did indeed do their best to put a stop to the horse but the rider had a nimble creature. The horse dodged the players' signals and with half of the Benson team and the rider in pursuit, the animal and Lottie rode into the flat landscape. The pitcher stood there and shook his head. He spat and threw his hat into the dirt.

The reverend and Caffee attempted to give chase but turned back and now rested on the bench. Jack and Shannon stood and looked into the distance. Shannon said, "Can't see them. That damn horse is headed for those mountains."

"I hate horses," Jack said. "Don't trust them. I been saying it."

Caffee grabbed his handkerchief from the front of his overalls. He removed his cap and whipped down his forehead. "You boys passing through?"

Jack said, "Yes, yes, sir. On the way to Californy. Can you point the way to boarding in this town?"

Caffee returned the handkerchief to his pocket and pressed this cap down on his head. "You passed a good number of them when you stepped off the train. Never had the pleasure of staying in Benson. So I'm afraid I wouldn't be of much help. Perhaps the reverend. Reverend?" The reverend's glasses glowed in the sun and his face darkened under the wide brim of his felt. He wore a thin mustache, not common in this country, and his left thumb had gone missing.

He put his finger to his chin. "Let me see," the reverend said. "I can recommend to you gentlemen the Virginia or the Grand Central, both right down by the station. You should find them to your liking."

Jack tipped his hat. "Much obliged, Reverend."

"No trouble. What awaits you in California?"

"Ranches. I mean, ranch work. We're partners looking to buy a ranch."

Caffee said, "Best of luck to you. Nice to meet you boys." He made his way over to the Bisbee side of the field, where the team gathered under the presumption that the game would be called if horse and lady did not return promptly.

The reverend stepped closer to Shannon and looked up at Jack, who still stood in the stands. "You gentlemen need any other advice or help come on down to the Methodist church. I'll be sure to help the best I can. Now if you will excuse me."

"Reverend," Shannon said.

"Yes?"

"What distinguishes the two?"

The reverend passed Shannon and without turning he said, "The Central has a bar." They watched him walk off into a stiff wind that began to pick up. Jack looked above him, as if he could see it. The reverend held his hat and leaned into the wind. His black overcoat blew behind him.

Jack said, "Well?"

Shannon shielded his eyes from the wind. "The Central. By a nose."

Down Fourth Street the sun began to touch the west. The east crept into darkness, with clouds stretching over mountains and curving across the broken granite that lined the peaks. The Grand Central hotel appeared in a blue coat of paint, about two days fresh. Jack said, "Classy." Shannon did not say if he agreed. The lobby was laid with linoleum and two palm trees flanked the desk where the clerk scribbled into a ledger. Two plush purple chairs sat across from the desk and a marble slab table hosted newspapers and trays awaiting ash. Piano drifted through the lobby. The bar could not be seen and Jack searched the place from the chair where he had helped himself to a seat. Shannon looked down at him.

Jack said, "Hell, you got all the money ain't, ye?"

Shannon searched his pockets for cigarettes but abandoned the effort after a number of inquiries about his person.

The clerk said, "Pleased to meet you. How can I be of service?" His skin was spotty and his balding head was tanned from the sun, which did not draw from the redness of his nose.

"We come on a recommendation from the reverend."

"Now which reverend would that be?"

Shannon looked back at Jack. "You happen to catch the reverend's name?"

Jack removed his hat and dropped it on the table. "Stump," he said. "The Reverend Stump."

Shannon nodded. "Stump. The Reverend Stump."

The man smiled. "Yes, I know the reverend. Awfully kind of him. He is a proud man. Lord bless him. Let me introduce myself. I'm Sam Friedman, the proprietor."

He shook Shannon's hand firm, leaving Shannon's hand moist in the palm. He wiped the moisture into his jeans and said, "We have come to stay the evening, Mr. Friedman. Any vacancies?"

Friedman looked down at his ledger. "Let me see. Let me see. Oh why, yes. Yes, we do. A double room or two singles?"

"A double will do. Does it come with bath?"

"Bath, bath. Oh, yes. Yes. Complimentary." The man scribbled in his book. "Can I ask you to sign the registry, please?" He placed the registry on the counter with pen presented flat upon it.

Shannon looked back at Jack. "Come on and make your mark."

Shannon put his face close to the paper and signed Charles Dunlap. Jack made an X. The man revolved the ledger and said, "Thank you, Mr. Dunlap and Mr. ... huh ... Well, thank you, gentleman. Room three on the second floor. Enjoy your stay."

Jack said, "Where would a man find the bar if he was inclined?"

"Oh, yes, yes, just under the stairs, gentlemen. There you will find the door. Plenty of what you wish for but I'm afraid no gambling. City ordnance for hotels, you see?"

Jack's head hit the pillow and his hat hit the dark smooth floor rolling to the side of the claw tub and rested there. Shannon sat in front of the mirror rolling a cigarette. A ceramic vase filled with water stood on the polished desk and a bowl awaiting the contents of such. He poured the water into the wide bowl and draped an ivory towel over his shoulder. He rubbed the stubble on his neck and passed his hand over his face. He said, "I hardly took a bath in two years. Hell, maybe three. Now, I have the chance to take two in as many days."

Jack sat up. "Trouble is you don't smell any better for it. Ye got extra tobacco?"

Shannon cupped the water over his face. "The Lord helps those who help themselves." Shannon tossed the pouch over to Jack, landing on his chest.

Jack let the pouch sit before going to work. "I'm tired. I'm tired. A tired man needs a bed. The Lord is smiling on this fool 'cause he's got him one." Jack licked the paper with quick stabs of his tongue. He lit the cigarette and tossed back the pouch, missing the desk. Jack said, "Ye just 'bout out of it."

Shannon rubbed the towel over his face and sat in a red chair. He threw his feet up on the desk. "Not too old for a night out?"

Jack had his eyes closed. He lifted his head. "What ye reckon?"

"Bucking the tiger. What else, Jack?"

"Oh now, I'm sick of it. Shannon, I'm just too damn sore to do much of anything. Ye get out and I'll just mope round the saloon downstairs."

Shannon rose and pulled his jacket off the chair. "Suit yourself."

Jack propped up on his elbows and let the cigarette dangle from the corner of his mouth. Ash hung in his beard. "Leave a few for old Jack. I'll take care of myself."

Shannon reached into his vest pocket and eyed the contents. "Half dollar on the desk for you, Jack. If you want more you'll have to win it."

"You got enough for ye person, I reckon?"

Shannon faced the mirror and with care set his hat like a crown on his head. "You know me, Jack, me boy. I make do." Shannon made for the door.

"Shannon," Jack called.

Shannon looked back.

"Good luck."

When Jack woke he was alone. The cigarette had singed his beard below his lip and he wiped off a long line of ash that led to a sore spot on his lip. The room was bright with the smell of burning oil and a strong flame burned in the lantern on the desk. He searched the bed around him before he sat up. The window displayed a clear night punctuated by a high moon, stark in the sky over Fourth. A horse pulling a cart rattled below. Washing his face over the sink, the music came to his ear. The piano in the bar was still haunting the hotel and he examined his burnt lip in the mirror before descending the stairs. He ran his hand on the railing and stepped purposefully down. Friedman was dusting the palm trees there in the lobby and watched Jack make his way to the center of the room. A chandelier hung from the ceiling and Jack stood looking above him. Friedman said, "Beauty ain't she?"

"I somehow missed it when I walked in."

"From St. Louis. Same steel from the Wainwright Building forged her. Floated it down the Mississippi and onto a train. Here she is. I like to think it holds the place together." Friedman put down the feather duster and put his hands in the crook of his back. "Can I interest you in some supper?"

Jack looked past Friedman and across the street. The miner stood asleep against a tree, across the girth of Fourth. Jack passed Friedman and ducked slightly. He pointed. "Ye see that man across the way there?"

Friedman squinted. "Yes, I do."

"You know that man? I reckon he's been following me."

Sam looked again. "Oh, dear. Yes. Yes. I know that man. That is poor Charles Fink. I'm afraid that man is not all with us. He come in from the Rincon with another man. I believe not too long now. Brought with him a lion. Never seen one like it. Still hanging in Castaneda's store for all to wonder upon. Yes, about nine feet. You might not believe a beast as such roams those mountains. But you be sure never to roam yourself out in that wilderness. Anyhow, he's been here since just roaming the town. He's not harming anyone so the sheriff hasn't been inclined to have him move on. I wager the time is nigh for poor Fink."

Jack said, "And what of the other man?"

Friedman put his finger to his chin. "Now what was that man's ... Oh, oh. Westerliche. Yes, that's the name. Well. I can't say I know. I only seen him once. Not since they hung that lion up. But I'll be happy to call upon the sheriff if that man has been set on harassing a patron of mine. We can't have it in this town. They don't stand for it in Tucson and we can't stand for it here."

Jack brushed his beard. "Now, now. No need to involve the sheriff. He ain't done nothing to me. Just keep seeing him is all."

"Suit yourself," said Friedman. "But the offer stands."

Jack tipped his hat. "Very kind of you. Now, if you will excuse me. The bar is calling."

Friedman smiled. "Your friend left to find himself some other forms of entertainment. Have a nice night." Jack found his way under the stairs.

Lanterns hung from long nails in the wall. The bar was short with three stools and little standing room to speak of. The piano next to the bar stood silent, as one had to crank it for a play. The saloon was empty save the barman who stood in blue denim shirt and apron. The long, pointed beard he wore was beginning to grey, reminding Jack of an old friend in a long-lost mining camp. His eyes bulged in a head shrunken and wrinkled from time and labor. A picture of McKinley hung crusted over behind the bar. Next to it a jar of corn whiskey with snake coiled inside, snug in eternal slumber. Jack pulled a stool and the barman stood hands folded over his chest.

"Help ye?" he said.

"Hope so. I seem to recall the proprietor saying a man could wet his throat in here." Jack looked past the barman. "Problem is, I don't make out much of nothing back there except that poison ye guarding."

"The proprietor is damn fool. You can quote me on that if ye wish."

Jack took his hat off and placed it on the bar. "I ain't here to take any sworn statements or have a man raise his hand to the Lord Almighty. I'm fixing for a drink. Can you oblige?"

The barman ran his gums over his bottom lip. "I damn sure can serve ye up mescal or this snake juice ye eyeing."

"Who said I was eyeing it?"

"Ain't no one said it. I just did."

Jack studied the barman. "You mean to tell me I got a choice between cactus juice and that there snake piss?"

"Ye catch on quick."

Jack sat back on the stool and shook his head. "Hell. Serve'em up then."

The barman pulled two glasses from behind the bar and Jack said, "Help ye self to one." He pulled a third and lined them up like soldiers. The barman poured the snake whiskey first. It ran like syrup into the glass and the snake uncoiled with the tilt of the bottle. He next grabbed a blue bottle from the shelf and a golden mescal filled the second and third empty glasses. Jack grabbed the snake whiskey and said, "What do ye drink to?"

"I don't drink to nothing. Never did."

Jack raised the snake whiskey. "To nothing then." The men drank. Jack looked hard at the empty glass. "This here makes a man want to hiss. Hell. Drank them all. The sand whiskey on the trail. Taos Lighting round Santa Fe but never had the likes of that."

The man poured another. "Have it again so ye don't forget."

Jack shot the snake whiskey. "Damn to hell."

The mescal went down like candy water from a cool spring after the snake spirit. The barman folded his hands over his chest and stood back from the bar. Jack stepped off the stool and up into the doorway and said, "Ye a credit to the profession." The barman spat into a bucket between his feet and sucked his bottom lip.

The chandelier had dimmed and the feather duster sat alone on the marble table with Freidman nowhere in sight. The piano kicked up again. Jack stepped onto the boardwalk and leaned up against the post of the hotel. Fink was gone. The moon cast a yellow halo under all below. Sharp shadows lined the buildings and men stood in darkness, mulling around the depot and fading into the station's shadow. Jack watched them from his distance as they faded in and out of the moonlight. He moved on and tucked his hands into his coat pocket raising the collar on his thin coat. A wagon passed carrying slaughtered beef. A trail of blood followed pooling in spots. Dogs clicked their tongues lapping at the puddles that reflected the face of the moon.

Jack stopped in saloons and drank with miners and field hands and gamblers and horsemen carrying colts and knives buckled to boot. A man passed him whiskey whose hand hosted three fingers on each. His nails were long, sharp, green. His eyes swollen purple. He spoke of events in the eastern territory. Jack nodded along and after two drinks, moved on. He stuck his head into gambling halls but did not see Shannon and did not linger further. A wide clearing marked the El Paso and Southwestern depot. The moon glow off the pitched roof took on the appearance of a cathedral in the middle of a desolate, besieged wasteland. Few creatures moved at this far end. Jack sat across the clearing and rested on a stoop leading to a burnt skeleton of a building. Wilted flowers lay crumbling inside the charred doorframe. The stars speckled in the sky above him. His head bobbed to the song of the cosmos and he whistled the tune and laughed at his drunken thoughts.

In the distance he heard the rattling of harness and jingles of metal and glass and what sounded to be the jostling of minute bells. Jack searched the distance and saw nothing to the right, which gaped into the ink of the wilderness. He looked toward the station. The sound became tighter. He sat up. From the left a shape grew from the darkness and there shadows formed a mule of unusual stock. A white line ran down the snout of the animal, drawn by a wide thumb. Behind the mule, a wagon of four wide wheels, carrying wooden boxes stamped with ports of New Orleans and San Francisco. A sack filled with feathers found place in the back of the cart. Over rocks the cart shook and feathers floated off the load rocking gently down behind. The moon outlined the rider and his great-brimmed hat, stretching like a plateau from the mountain of his high crown. His white shirt and hair came radiant toward Jack and he stood to witness this vision wheel past him.

The rider called, "Whoa!" He pulled the rein high and the mule brayed and came to a dead stop in front of Jack. "Damn near ran you over! Somehow missed you standing there. Hold on," he said. The light struck his face and his leather skin glistened as sandpaper or quartz might. His grin was slight. He dismounted from the vessel, rounded the front of the mule and rubbed the beast's snout. "Hello," he said.

"How do ye do?" Jack returned.

The Indian stood before him and tipped his hat. His face was short and he wore a long chin with the hair to match the feature. His pants were muddy in the knees, but his shirt was otherwise clean and ties held the cloth in place of buttons. He had a scar down his face. His eyebrow bore the mark of the instrument's downward swipe. His eye opposite the scar hung slightly. He pulled a pack of Durham's out of his breast pocket and said, "Tobacco?"

"Kindly," Jack said.

The Indian felt his pockets and with cigarette in mouth, he grunted and reached into the wagon and pulled out a thick box of matches. "Fire," he said. He struck the match with his thumb and stretched his arm toward Jack's face. Jack puffed into the flame. Jack exhaled. The Indian puffed and shook the match. He said, "They call me Muldoon."

"Jack. They call me Jack."

Muldoon said, "Sit."

Jack took his place on the stoop and Muldoon sat next to him, cigarette in lip, blowing smoke into the stars. There was silence. Jack watched the movement of the constellations along with Muldoon. Jack stamped out his cigarette and said, "Live in town?" Muldoon drew another cigarette from the pack, lit it with the end of his and passed it to Jack.

"No. Leaving."

Jack said, "I gather a good time for that."

Muldoon studied Jack and from the spot where the matches had been produced, he pulled a bottle of corn whiskey. He removed the cork with his teeth and placed it in his front pocket. He dragged from the bottle and motioned toward Jack. Muldoon said, "For Bisbee."

Jack dragged on his cigarette. "Myself, I'm headed somewhere." Silence came again and the pulls off the bottle echoed against the station across the clearing and back toward the dark desert abyss. Jack said, "You in Bisbee then?"

Muldoon stood and brushed the mane of the mule with his hand. He shook his head. "I am yoemem. From Rio Yaqai. From Bisbee I return to the Sierra Madre." He tilted his head toward the wagon and waved his hand toward the wooden crates stacked and tied with hemp. "This will hold us when we make the next stand against the Mexicans." Jack sat still. His mouth was dry and he tried to inhale but the smoke seemed to stick to the sides of his mouth. Muldoon put his boot up on the step and rocked into his stance. Jack noticed the rusty handle of a dagger rising from his boot. Muldoon continued, "The fight will not end. My father fell in Bacum. Brother in Bacatete. I will fall and join them. I will not live as slave."

Jack said, "I reckon no man should." Muldoon stared into Jack's eyes. Jack broke the stare and threw his cigarette. Something scampered from under the steps and along the sides of the stoop.

When he turned back, Muldoon still looked upon him and said, "Have you ever killed a man?" Muldoon drew another cigarette and passed it to Jack.

Jack looked at the cigarette in his hands. "Ye have them matches?"

Muldoon again drew his thumb over the head of a match and said, "In Hacienda La Poza, I met man. He rode in and lingered for days. He kept to the hill at night. Building large fires. Around the fire he would drink. Drink and talk. He rode from south Colorado, he claimed. He talk of riches. Riches and fate. He had long, sharp knife. At night, around the fire, he would sharpen sticks he gathered in scrub. Burn them in fire. I would sit. Drink whiskey. Smoke cigarettes. I watched him. His stories of riches. Fate. Cards. His final night came. He got very drunk. Finished all his whiskey and he told of the payroll from Guaymas. The payroll to the Colorado mine. The mine where yoemem slave. He wanted partner and answer by the time of sunrise. I watched him from across the fire. He smiled and went to sleep. Early that morning as the sun came over ridge. I took his knife and drove it into his chest. I dragged his body to boulder field. There black vulture waited for him. With wings toward the sun. I lingered for half the morning then rode off into Sonora." Jack folded his hands. His elbows on knees. Muldoon said, "Keep whiskey." He rounded the mule and climbed into the coach and grabbed the reins. He looked down at Jack. "To Bisbee," he said, sending a shake down the greasy leather and the mule lunged forward. The wagon rolled and bumped back into the blackness it arrived from.

The walk back to the hotel was a fever dream. He left the empty whiskey bottle spinning in the dirt after stumbling into a hitching post. A figure in front of a darkened grocery shook his head and spat. Jack thought he was drooling. He thought he was sweating. He then figured both. The opera house came into view and was dressed in bulbs of light. Outside banjos and fiddles accompanied vaudevillians in blonde wigs and a woman naked in her midsection danced and clapped cymbals. Boys fidgeted at the edge of the crowd and sang. He moved on. Under a dim electric current, he looked up on a monster with claws drawn and ready to tear the flesh from a victim. Jack ran his fingers through the thick coat of the animal. The golden fur of the cat was as if spun from the finest silk. The eyes missing, boiled and eaten as a delicacy to obtain the prowess of the beast. But the eyes fixed on Jack were of the human species. The figure across the way. Jack did not look but saw the movement in the glass of Castaneda's supply. The figure stayed at a distance. The clamping of his boots on the boardwalk ticked like a clock on a desert monastery wall. No attempt to hide the pace or existence of such.

The hotel lobby was bright as much as it was empty. The feather duster was gone and there now sat a small empty chair by the stairs. Jack stopped in front of the clerk's desk, the ledger open with a pen in the binding. A single name after his mark. That of Tobias Morrison. Jack watched the empty lobby as he ascended the stairs. The room was untouched. The blankets pulled as he had left them and the basin still filled with the soapy gray water. He searched his pockets but did not recall for what cause. The mirror was blurred and patches of light danced in the reflection. He sat on the bed and reached down to remove his boots.

When he awoke on the floor, he rolled his head slowly and flipped onto his stomach. He could not recall if the door was ajar due to the fact he did not close it. He dragged himself up, turned the handle and softly closed the door. The window was still a black mirror. Jack steadied himself on the desk and poured the water from the vase into his mouth. It ran down the sides of his face and into his shirt. His sleeve was the towel he reached for. His head heavy from drink, he traced the drops of water on the desk and there sat one US dollar bill. Jack stared at the face on the paper and then turned and searched the room. The closet hid no garments. Under the bed was nothing. The tub sat dry. Jack sat at the edge of the bed. He held the bill up to the light and flipped it back and forth, inspecting the currency, the vase of water wedged between his legs. He raised the vessel and emptied the remnants. Jack ran his fingers through his beard, folded the bill and tucked it into his shirt pocket.

At the desk sat a decrepit gentleman in a suit too large for his frame and that of his disposition. He rolled his lips in a circular motion, in such a way that did not cease. His hat bore him the respect his suit failed him. Jack stopped and tipped his hat. "Howdy there, old-timer."

The old man said, "Can I help you?"

"What time ye have there?"

The man arched down and lifted the timepiece close to his eye. "Five. Five in the a.m."

"Quiet, I suppose."

"I reckon to be true. Fact though quiet ain't the norm. Never is. Got word from young Phillip some fool done try to kill oneself. Drank something he hoped on sending him to meet the Lord. Was that boy been hanging around from the hills. Said he saw the devil."

Jack said, "Who said that."

"Who?"

"Who said they saw the devil?"

"Ye done confuse me now. Don't know if the fool said it or young Phillip. Any man fixin' to drink some demon juice seen the devil, I reckon."

"That man Fink?"

The man lifted his hat. "Mister, can't remember last time I been asked as many inquiries." He rolled his lips over his gums and sat looking at Jack.

"The miner. Was it the miner?"

"Don't right know what the fella does for a living."

Jack said, "Thank you for ye time."

"Suit yourself."

The depot steamed and iron moans and hisses filled the space between freight cars. The water station hung like gallows above the lines of boxcars filled with oranges and celery. The foul smell of wet horse was everywhere. They stomped and grunted on the planks of the cattle cars. Jack stepped with purposeful footfall under the steely giants, his hands in his pockets and hat low over his brow. He stopped when he heard voices and ducked under cars when he felt a presence near. The grease off the rods stained the sleeve of the purple jacket he wore. He felt foolish when he tried to brush it off. Voices moved down along the rails and Jack steadily inched from under the freight car to affirm their clearance.

He rose to find the door of a car halfway pulled open. Crates filled with beets blocked the passage up. The grab iron was cool to the touch and he pulled himself up and in between the wall and produce. He shimmied to the back with his nose rubbing against the wood and roots. The musk of cool fresh earth dangled over the crates. The crude path led to a clearing in the front of the car, where two men sat with legs stretched and backs to cargo. A scratchy voice said, "Hey, bo. Join on in."

Jack came around and stood in front of the pair. Slivers of light crept into the car and the man on the left said, "Howdy there, cowboy." The voice leaned forward and Shannon's eyes glowed in the dust-ridden morning shine.

6: PANTANO STATION

"Have a seat, friend," said the old hobo.

"Don't mind if I do." Jack inspected the area and sat upon it.

The hobo continued, "They call me Tomato Can. Tomato Can Tommy, that is. Picked up the name up in yards back in Albany. Too long now to remember why. Guessin' it had to do with a tomato can."

"Pleasure," Jack said. He looked at Shannon, whose face was dressed in the gloom of the train. He pulled strands from a bed of straw that lay beneath him.

Tomato Can looked over at Shannon. "Oh, this here is Charles. He an old friend now." Tomato Can laughed. "Old friend, he is. He don't talk much from what I gather but that ain't a complaint from a bo."

Shannon threw a piece of straw in the air and the three men watched it fall between them. Jack said, "Charles?" Shannon said nothing.

Tomato Can said, "He don't talk much do he? I told ye he don't say much. I take it he talks when he drinks."

Jack nodded and spat. "I can take that as fact." Jack dragged himself backward. "Excuse me. You don't mind I'll get me some shut-eye. If ye don't mind there, Charles?"

Tomato Can said, "Charles? Old Charles don't mind."

Shannon said, "Best to keep it down till we leave the depot, Tommy. Aye?" Tomato Can put his finger to his lips and shook his head in deep agreement.

The men sat in that quiet and dank place. Footsteps and slamming doors sent vibrations through the car. Knocking was heard and then stopped. Yells and a whistle. When the car jerked forward, the crates began to tremble and Tommy rocked on his straw cushion. Shannon stood. "Go on and check on that door," he said to Tommy.

Tommy rose and stepped back with quickness and said, "Yup. Seeing daylight." Shannon smiled and groaned as he sat.

Jack noticed the sack that lay beside Shannon. Jack said, "Is them ye possibles?" Shannon eyed the bag and said nothing.

Tommy hit the vibrating floor with his fist. "Them is possibles all right. Them there is riches." Tommy giggled with apparent pride at the contents. Shannon put his hand on the bag and he shifted the position of the thing.

Jack said, "What's to share in that bag there, Charles?"

"Jack, this here bag is the property of one Charles and his partner Tommy here."

Tommy hopped up on his hands. "Yes, sir. We stole it fair and square."

Jack ran his fingers down the hair on his chin. "You stole it did ye?"

Shannon looked over at Tommy.

Tomato Can said, "Oh, come now. Old Jack here ain't gonna run us in. Ain't that right, Jack?"

"That I can give my word on. Tommy, tell me something, if ye don't mind? Did you do the dirty work while Charles here stood silent?"

Tommy shook his head. "No, no. Ain't got the nerve for it. All I'm much good for is keeping watch out for the law or bulls. This time was no different. Old Charles had the fool picked out already. A man with a faro bank should be hell of a lot more careful. That there is his business he carrying around with him." Tommy scratched the grey and knotty hair under his tweed hat. "I can't help but wonder if the fool woke up yet. Quite a knock ye gave there, Charles. Quite a knock."

Jack removed his hat and shook his hair. He groaned. "You killed him didn't you, Shannon? Or whatever ye name is?" Tommy searched Jack for meaning and he turned to Shannon with the same such question in his eyes.

Shannon looked at Tommy. "Sorry, Tomato Can." He rose and he peered through a hole in the boards of the car. The passing yellow landscape wiped across that terrain with only the valley walls darkened by the coming day.

Tommy said, "Why you call him Shannon and Charles what the hell you apologizing for?" Shannon locked his arm and steadied himself as the train stumbled over an old section of track.

Jack said, "Watch yourself. You might just get hurt."

Shannon laughed and started to cough. "Jack, you, man, have finally done it. Gave your old friend a good laugh. I certainly needed it."

"So, you two know each other now?"

Shannon said, "Yes, Tommy. Quite our fortune Jack here climbed aboard our ship and joined back into the ranks from which he attempted to flee."

"Flee?" Jack pulled the dollar from his breast pocket and held the bill aloft. Waving the bill in the air, he said, "And I suppose you have no recollection of this? Your intentions was clear."

"Mother always said I bore a soft heart. And do you still wish to depart our company?"

"Ye damn right," Jack said. "When this train stops I'll be looking to make my disappearance. Damn if I get hung over ye greed." Shannon walked over and squatted in front of Jack. The car now filled with beams of sharp light and the dry heat of the morning.

Shannon said, "Now I can't recall you voicing much objection when you picked out that jacket there. That shirt or the pants, for that matter."

"Well, I can tell ye this much," Jack said. "This here is my voice. This here is my objection." Jack tore the dollar bill crossways and once more tossing the four pieces above his head, each fluttering to the floor as if butterflies alit on a flower.

Shannon stood, "So noted."

"Tommy," Jack said. "You give a second thought to the fact there may be a posse waiting at whatever godforsaken stop this train is on the way to? This man here has left a trail of blood down this line. God knows what else he pulled before I ran into him. Ye can't run forever. They catch up to men like you."

Tommy looked at Shannon. "So ye ain't Charles, is ye?"

"No, Tommy. The name is not Charles. Don't matter much now what it is to you."

Tommy swallowed. His mouth was dusty. Throat parched. He said, "Lord, what have ye done?"

Jack said, "Say them prayers, Tommy. You need them now. We all do."

The train picked up speed. The open door did not offer much wind past the barrier of crates separating them from the world outside. A festering heat gripped the air inside the space. The men sat apart from each other, as if the distance would foster a wind. The vessel bobbed up and down on the packed desert earth. Tommy nodded off just when the whistle began to blow long calls. He jumped and before gaining his bearing, fell over. He pressed his eye to the south-facing wall of the car and proclaimed, "There she is."

Jack walked over. "There what is?"

"The Arizona and South Eastern. Coming up from Bisbee and Douglas. She crosses the line here." Tomato Can turned to Shannon. "We approaching."

Shannon rubbed the two-day stubble on his chin and looked up at Jack.

Jack said, "What exactly do you mean we approaching? Approaching what?"

Shannon sat mute.

The car took on a growling vibration as the Northbound drew closer.

Tommy said, "The caves."

"The what?"

Tommy yelled, "The caves!"

157

The train began to slow, and Jack put his back to the wall and stared over at Shannon on the other side of the car. Tommy said, "At the signal. Looks like we have the right of way." The dull bell could be heard in the distance and grew sharp as the car passed.

Jack walked over. "Shannon, what caves is he talking about?"

Tommy said, "Caves not far from Vail. Three or four miles from memory. Plenty of room to hide out while we split the take. No way we have that on our person heading into Tucson."

Jack returned to the wall, next to Tomato Can. "And how you come by these caves?"

"I was serving a vag charge in Pima. Guard there told me 'bout them and after release, a yegg buddy and me staked the grounds out. Just in case something came down to lay low. Here we is. In need. You can't paint a picture finer to fit."

Jack stared at Shannon. "You all plan to walk into that wilderness with no possibles? The hangman don't need to find ye. You both will perish."

Shannon said, "Tommy knows this country, Jack. He's walked these hills. He knows the springs."

"He speaks! I can tell you then, Shannon. Ye found yourself a real ringer in this here, Tomato Can Tommy. Hell. Albany. King of the desert. Just glad ye will be jumping off this train. I'm happy to be moving down the line without you."

Tommy perched himself back on the straw. He tilted his hat down over his eyes and tucked his chin into his shirt collar. Shannon took the same course. "It will be for the best, Jack. You never did have the nerve for the rails." Jack spat and stared up at the ceiling. Tommy began to snore.

Jack kicked Shannon's foot and Shannon clutched the burlap sack on his lap. "Wake time, boys. Get up. This train is stopping."

Tommy rose. "How long I been sleeping?"

"'Bout twenty minutes, I reckon."

"Damn, that for certain ain't Vail. Must be Pantano. Watering stop. Boiler must be low."

Jack put his hand on the wall and felt the vibration slowly beginning to wind down.

Jack whispered. "You said them prayers, Tommy?"

Steam released and the train shook to a stop. The scuffle of feet could be heard in the sand. Men were heard yelling. Jack and Tommy had their ears pressed to the wall. Jack looked down at Shannon and nodded his head toward the door and pointed. Tommy pressed his ear harder to the wall. The door slammed shut. Shannon jumped to his feet. A voice boomed from the door. "We know ya'll are in there. Right now we can't decide what in the hell to do with ye."

All three froze and in that wasteland of sound, every noise became pronounced and certain of place. A wind blew. The cooling of the rods cracked and reverberated in the car. Ears snapped to attention and eyes shifted in the grim faint of light. Feet moved in the sand and then nothing. Tommy shifted his right foot and the boards under him creaked as if a door unoiled for a century slowly shut on his fate. The voice said, "We knew you was in there. Ye might as well have a seat." Jack removed his hat. He placed it back on his head and sat. Shannon gripped the sack and removed two large stacks of bills, wrapped in paper and held with red tape. He put one each into his back pockets. Tommy eyed him.

The voice continued. "Ye hear in there? Now listen. We decided what to do with ye. We here is going to open this door. Ye come out slowly with ye hands over ye heads. Anything else we're liable to shoot ye down. Don't give us a reason 'cause we might just shoot for the hell of it. Now. When we open the door, that is when ya'll file out. Ye hear? Don't expect an answer. Just get to it." Jack looked over at Shannon and his eyes were calm. Jack wiped the sweat off his nose and nodded toward the door. The door rolled open and slammed to a stop. The voice ordered, "Get ye asses out here." Tommy moved first, after Shannon waved him forward. Along the back of the boxcar they inched slowly toward the wall of white light that awaited them. Tommy reached the edge of the car. "Jump down off of there." Tommy hit the floor and let out a wheeze after lifting himself off the ground.

"Now the next bastard."

Shannon jumped down.

"You line up. Put ye hands on the top of ye heads." Jack stood at the edge of the door. "What ye waiting for? Git on down here." Jack jumped and landed squat. "Looks like a damn monkey." The voice grabbed his arm and flung him into Shannon. "There is ye place. Put ye hands on ye head. That's right. On that greasy hat of yours."

Three stood guard. Two of the cowboys armed, one with rifle and the other with Colt pistol. The third, a Black brakeman in overalls, bore a confused expression on his face. "Three of them?" he said.

Jack said, "This hat ain't greasy."

The cowboy whose voice ordered them from the train said, "Come again?"

"This hat ain't greasy."

"Point taken. It ain't. But that fact ain't worth a damn. Dead men don't need hats." At that, Jack scrunched his lip toward his nose and snarled at the cowboy. The two gave off nothing more than being a set of ambitious hands from the Empire ranch. Each with eager eyes and ornate low-heel boots with loud jinglers, that revealed their presence with any movement about in the dirt. The voice wore a cropped

mustache, which betrayed his time spent somewhere in Baja
and his hand jerked with a suggestion of condition.

His partner said, "Nate, what we going to do with the
lot?"

The brakeman spoke up. "We due in Tucson in an hour.
We can't put them boys back on this train. Boss would throw
a right fit."

Nate looked at the brakeman, the brakeman at the partner. Nate, with gun fixed on the three pointed to the brakeman, said, "You. Go on and ask ye boss what he want to do
with these three. If I have to, I'll march them into Tucson
to git the reward. Don't give a damn too much about it." He
then nodded to his partner. "Billy, go on and fetch Heffner. I
believe yonder in the wash."

The brakeman quickly turned and ran toward the face of
the iron beast. The engineer could be seen in the distance with
hat in hand and awaiting word on the events. Billy backed up
slowly. His rifle held firm and sure in grip. "Don't trust any of
this lizard shit here, Nate. Don't trust a dust of them."

Nate shifted the gun in his hands and rolled his eyes to
meet the figure of the three men before him. He said, "No mind
to it. I won't move an eye off this lot. Go on. Fetch Heffner.
He'll know what to do with this collection of murderers."

Billy climbed a short rise and quickly returned leading
his horse. He toed the stirrup and gave one last look before
returning his rifle to the scabbard. Giving his horse the signal,

it kicked up a thick drifting cloud that passed over the prisoners, all standing with hands on top of their heads, seemingly consigned to their fate. The whistle gave off a short and high blow and when that cloud settled back down, there stood Nate with a knife protruding from the side of his neck and the wide-eyed look of a man staring into eternity.

Jack did not realize much of what was transpiring there before him. He heard a shout from the brakeman who was jumping up and down with the engineer at the front of the train. Shannon stepped back. Nate gurgled. Blood popped from his lips, running down his neck and underneath his shirt. The young cowboy stood frozen in the moment of his impending doom, with arm cocked and finger still ready for the signal to fire. Tommy said, "What in the hell?" his hands still flat on the top of his hat. Jack started to inch back.

Tommy said, "What you done, Charles?" Shannon stepped forward and grabbed Nate's hand. As if a medicine show puppeteer, Shannon pointed the gun at Tommy and put a single bullet through his forehead.

Jack screamed, "My goddamn ears!" Shannon let go of Nate's arm and there Nate fell and there he lay, only feet from the old hobo, flattened out and soaking in a pool of his own.

Jack raised his head. The brakeman and the engineer were gone. So was Shannon. The ringing in his ears sent him to the ground. The whistle blew two long screams. He searched the ground in hopes to discover a clue for the way to run. His hand banged into the firearm and Jack took hold of the Colt and shoved it into the seat of his belt. He stood, blood smeared on the front of his shirt. Toward the caboose he saw figures, maybe three, looking toward him.

"Jack! Jack! Up here!" The voice was from Shannon, who sat atop the dead man's horse. "Come on, you goddamn fool! Get up here." Jack ran up the sand embankment toward the water tower, where the horses had been tied. Shannon reached down and extended his hand. Jack wiped the sweat from his forehead. The blood beaded there in the folds.

Jack said, "Ye never told me ye could ride a horse."

"Quite the luck then to find out now. Are you coming, lad?"

"Hell, I ain't gonna take a bullet for ye."

"Then fast, man! Fast!" Jack grabbed his hand. Someone fired a shot.

"Aye, best to keep your head low." Jack fastened his hands around Shannon's waist and ducked his head under his left arm. Shannon turned the horse toward the hills of scrub. The horse sped through a cemetery, kicking up sacaton and salt grass. Then at a pace past a stone building where chickens scrambled and into a distance dotted with pink clouds.

7: THE CAVES

They rode through country of low scrub and young mesquite and ironwood that held branches toward the sky, like hands reaching toward salvation. The horse was of fit stock and took the terrain with a steady character in stride. Navigating outcrops and cuts of sandstone, the pair moved ever closer to the mountains that stood watching. Sweat ran into the creases of their eyes and heat shimmer shook the surrounding horizon. Hours passed since their escape and the men had spoken little since. The horizon showed no sign of pursuit and the ragged party nooned in a gulch dotted with mesquite and chinaberry. Jack collapsed after dismounting and struggled to remove his boots. He sat barefoot in a spring that fed the wash and dipped his lips into the shallow pools of cool water. Catching his breath, he spat out the sand caught under his tongue. After a short rest, Shannon explored further up the gulch and was gone for some time. Jack would have suspected abandonment had Shannon not left the animal behind. The horse mulled among the bush and picked at the grass quietly.

Jack took hold of the dead man's satchel and laid his possibles out for inspection. A half-full canteen, ammunition, matches, knife and jerky, from which Jack selected a soft piece and slowly sucked on the fat. He laid the dead man's firearm on the ground before him and inspected the worn but steady piece. When Jack heard Shannon making his way back, he tucked the pistol under his jacket. Shannon found Jack washing his long hair in the spring. When he stood to acknowledge Shannon's return, water ran off his hair. The drops sparkled and hung glistening in his beard. Jack shook his head. "I can't suppose what you wandered off to find. The next thing ye decide to pull will be of no surprise." Shannon rested his hand against a thick mesquite branch and rubbed his forehead into his arm. Jack continued, "Well? What was ye off doing then?"

"I happen to be patching together how to get out of this."

"And this here spring was a clue?"

Shannon removed his hat and hung it on a skinny branch that bobbed when he released his hold. "Thought perhaps it may lead to an opening."

"Opening?"

"The caves."

"The caves? You mean ye don't know where they are?"

Shannon knelt and cupped his hand to the water. "Aye, I have an idea. Three mile from Vail. Where we were planning to get off. From what we discussed. I figure."

"Ye figure?"

"Aye, ten mile or so." Shannon slurped the water from his hand.

Jack shook his head. "This heat is getting to ye. That there is the plan? Ten mile or so? You plan on wandering this desert in search of a hole in the ground, we might or might not find, while half of the territory might or might not be riding out to hang us?"

"That be the plan, Jack. That be the plan."

"And tell me why I should go along with it?"

"Because on foot alone in this desert you will die, Jack. That or be hung. You're too young to meet the Almighty. Not yet." Shannon walked over to him. "Together we have a chance. And as I said. We share. Half of this is yours." Shannon reached from his back pocket and pulled the paper-wrapped stack. "Five thousand, Jack. Five thousand. Here. Take it."

Jack stared at the dirty white paper that held his fortune. "I sure as hell ain't taking that blood money." He walked past Shannon and started to button his shirt, still wet from the wash in the spring. Shannon studied him and shoved the package back into his coat pocket. Jack continued, "When they pin us down, I'll make damn sure they hang you first."

"Jack, you won't let me forget it. I will hang first. I insist. Come on then. Gather up your belongings. We have riding to do."

They rode among hackberry. Their path cut through fields of volcanic rock, jutting from the crust of that desert like markers to these events. The horizon lay stretched with clouds and between the formations, the presence of a blue memory of the sky. The sun peeked out of the wide holes in the heavens above and fleeting shadows could be seen flung over the sides of foothills in the distance. They stopped and followed a dust cloud rise on the horizon and figures of cattle could be seen stretching and curved as the herd moved out. The cloud disappeared. With it came the slant of nightfall. Shannon settled on an outcropping to build the fire against. The tall figures shielded any light from an eager party traveling by night to make time. Jack walked through catclaw and picked at twigs to gather for fire. Shannon patted the horse and removed the saddle. He poured water from the dead man's canteen into his hat and watered the animal. Shannon took a deep gulp from the canteen and called for Jack to drink up.

Under a saguaro that bore the likeness of a cross, Jack collected dry droppings of paloverde and he walked to the tree and ran his hand through the flowers that bloomed yellow. Bees worked into the petals. A sparrow hawk sat perched in the upper reaches and stared off into the mountain peaks, holding vigil to the secret folds of the earth's memory. Jack returned to the outcropping and dropped the small pile he collected onto the kindling. With the supply, Shannon began to mold a bird's nest.

Jack pointed, "Look yonder."

"What?" Shannon rose and followed Jack's hand toward the ridges of limestone that ran slanted onto the desert floor. There a column of black speckles emptied into the dusk of that world. Behind those creatures, the sky morphed into fuchsia and they disappeared like smoke into the hue and shadow of the belching rock.

Jack said, "There's your hole."

A ringtail searched the pockets of the satchel in the night. Torn paper that held the dead man's jerky supply lay strewn through the camp. The air was clear and the smell of dirt and sand bled into the silence of the morning. Jack warmed his face in the rising sun. His skin swollen, with red burned into his cheeks. Jack sat cross-legged on a flat rock, his eyes closed and palms pressed into the earth and he felt the yawn of the planet. The dirt over the fire was brushed off and Shannon looked over the ashes gathered there to inspect for smoke.

Jack said, "No smoke but a tracker worth half his salt would pick the trail up from here."

Shannon looked around the camp. "Then let's be on our way before he comes around."

The horse followed a break in the low scrub that led along the limestone ridges of the foothills. Shannon pointed the horse toward the toothed mountain, where creatures fled from its belly the night before. The underbrush shook and out ran two jackrabbits.

Jack patted Shannon's shoulder. "Stop the horse. Stop the horse," he whispered.

Shannon said, "What you?"

Jack dismounted, reached into the back of his jacket and drew the gun from his belt. He took a knee and set a bead. The rabbit froze just before approaching a boulder and then was nothing more. Jack fetched the animal. Shannon tipped the brim of his hat, to the line of his hair.

Jack said, "Dinner. Can't make much of a fuss in this bush."

"Aye," said Shannon, "I see you to be the armed member of this party." Jack slipped the pistol back under his jacket. He mounted the horse and said nothing. Shannon looked back. "What do you intend to do with that weapon?"

"Well, tonight I fed your ass with it. Don't worry. I'll drive off any Indians if they come looking for ye scalp. Now git. Find ye hole."

The rabbit's neck was wrapped with a leather tie pinned to the saddle and the limp body slapped against the hinds of the horse, leaving a blood trail that dripped down the leg of the steed. The horse led them into a caldera that descended into a valley scattered with saguaro and low, dry scrub. At the bottom, a spring gurgled that showed no human signs but was littered with rabbit and coatimundi track pressed into the soft sand. They stopped to drink, along with the horse. Shannon stood. "Must be near. Must be near." He walked again and called back. "What do you make of these?" He pulled a short, dented pot from under a thorn bush.

Jack inspected the find. "On account of this spring here. I venture this has seen a share of foot over these years." He turned the pot over. "This don't look too old now. See this here. Game trails all here." Jack pointed. "There. There. Huntin' likely."

The noon hours were spent under a desert willow that shook in a slight wind and they sat in the shadow of that tree, with cantina passed not more than twice. Jack caught himself in a short, sweaty sleep that he shook from. The party did not travel more than a few miles before the valley began to fade into a pink darkness, with solitary bats arising early to perform a dance on that painted stage. Scampering up unsteady terrain and each took turn on the reins, leading the horse up the steepening country. They hacked through twisted piñon and the effort put them before the mouth of a wide cave. Bats darted high above their heads, with number increasing by the moment. Shannon slapped Jack on the arm with the back of his hand. "Back to the horse," he said walking past him. Shannon removed the saddle and satchel from the animal and set them on the ground. He turned the horse around and slapped the back hind of the animal.

Jack said, "What to do with it?"

Shannon studied the area and led the horse to a syc-
amore, where he tied the animal to a branch of the tree.
Shannon rubbed the horse between the ears and said, "We
bid farewell." The horse stood watching the men made way
back up the scree toward the cave and did not lower its head
to chew on scrub until their footfall washed into the cooling
atmosphere. The pair kicked past the fallen piñon and stood
on the lip of the cave. Shannon adjusted the satchel over his
shoulder and stepped into the blackness.

Jack struck a match, lighting the makeshift torch he
fashioned of piñon bark and handkerchief that would guide
them through the narrow passage. The way forward was only
as wide a man could hope to fit. Flutters sounded overhead
in the void above them. Soon the light from the torch illuminated the inside of a wide chamber. Stalactites pointed
toward them from above and cast warped shadows against
the far wall of the chamber. The air was balmy with the dull
smell of sulfur. Jack dropped the extra wood he was carrying
and set to building the beginnings of a fire. Shannon stood
with torch in hand and lifted it toward the limestone ceiling.
The flame glowed white on the wall and Shannon ran his fingers over the markings of an ancient message. Beasts of all
sizes and manner were etched in black soot. Arcane circles,
drawn black and dotted, stretched across the drip curtain.

Shannon felt his way down the cavern wall. The burning
handkerchief began to ash and peel off dropping fire on the
cave floor. In near pitch darkness, he tumbled forward and fell,
his boot kicking over a bucket there in the rounded corner.

The sound echoed in the dark spaces of the cavern and tumbled down the deep corridors of the cave. Shannon stopped to inspect the contents spilled from the bucket. Jack was still fixing the kindling, when he looked up at a blistering light that shone above him. "Where all did you find that?" Shannon knelt and placed a long, thick candle beside him and set fire to the wick with the candle he was holding. The new light set an orange glow on the walls around them. Jack sat back and drew his legs inward, wrapping his arms around them.

Jack took a deep breath, spat and said, "Here I am. Back in a damn hole on the side of a mountain. Hell, I ditched Shakespeare to get out of a damn hole. Here I am. Back in one." He took off his hat and tossed it off to his side.

Shannon studied the walls after lodging the candle down a crack in the floor. "Aye, almost forgot." Shannon rose and from his back pocket removed the wrapped package. "This is yours now. Five thousand. Don't worry, lad. You don't have to count it." Shannon tossed the package and there it dropped in front of Jack. He looked down at the thing but other than his eyes, he made no motion to possess it. A deep tone rang through the cave and passed through the way they came. The men looked above them. Shannon said, "The mountain is calling, Jack. She's singing."

Jack removed his jacket, withdrew his gun and piled them to his right. "I've heard my share of strange inside holes. Can't count on this one being much different." Shannon lit another candle and wedged it down between two rocks. The shadows cloaked his cheeks and forehead, his sockets round with black circles and his pupils reflecting the three candles that burned motionless in the cavern.

Shannon said, "Have you thought of your plans, Jack?"

Jack spat. "My plans?"

"Aye, your plans now that you are a man of the upper crust."

"To be honest with ye. On thoughts I have given attention to? Those regard how the hell I'm gonna get out of this territory without a noose around my neck."

Shannon laughed. "Jack, Jack, an old dog like you worried about our escape? We make for Tucson. Two days walk." Shannon waved his hand over his head. "It's no cow town, Jack. We come in through the desert. Few, if any will notice. On straight to the depot."

"And they won't be looking for two fools in the desert?"

Shannon rubbed his heel into the cave floor. He exhaled. "Jack, we do not have much choice in the matter. We roll the die here. We either make it or ..."

"Or bust," Jack said.

"So be it. So start pondering your dream, Jack. If your number comes up, you will have to do something with that money."

"A shame to blow it in some gin hole on the Barbary." Jack laughed.

"Oh, that would be a matter of opinion."

"Yourself would eat all the oysters in the bay. Is them ye plans?"

"Me? No. No." Shannon laughed and rubbed his eye with the palm of his right hand. "Me. I have an old score to settle. One point of pride, Jack. Off to Tulsa. First train I can ride. And you know what, Jack? I plan on paying for the ticket. Well spent. Coin well spent. To see the look on that bastard's face. Coin well spent, indeed." Shannon rose and walked just beyond the light of the candles. Jack stared into that blankness. The impression of the flame danced on his retinas. He closed them tight, rubbing them. Shannon faded back into the light and there he took a knee at that edge.

Jack said, "You was off in Willcox that night. There was one man there at some saloon. Bought me a few. Had me drunk. His skin was like leather. With these great big eyes like the moon full. In them I could just tell he seen everything there was to see. He seen it. He rode the Great Northern, he told me. Caught it up in Cheyenne and rode it all the way to the ocean. What was his name? Damn all. Heavy drink that night. Don't recall his name. Now, might have been Ickerman. Anyway. He told me of the fir trees there on the coast. How the rain holds on the end of the needles. A million of them. The sun comes up and each one sparkles like a star. And the sea air. The sea air he spoke of. The thickness of it. The smell of the sea and pine. And the sun coming down like a blanket over all of it. Never seen that. I aim to though."

Jack sent his thoughts into the candle flame and across from him Shannon sat in silence and pulled at the hair that hung near his earlobe. Shannon knelt and grabbed two candles from the box. Lighting one from a candle on the floor, Shannon stuck the other down his pocket. "Wait here," he said.

Jack looked up, "Where in the hell are ye going?"

"On watch for fires. You want to come?"

Jack stared at him. "No."

"I figured as much. Then wait here." Shannon followed the light toward the slabs. The light disappeared down the passageway and Jack stared up at the vaulted stalagmites that hung far above him. He kicked the kindling and again began to make the fire. The piñon smoked at first, but he blew into the dry grass and a small flame came from the only sizable branch he carried in with him. He examined the dead man's gun as he did in the gulch. Jack released the cylinder and shook into his palm the four remaining bullets. He held the bullets up to the fire and turned them in the light and reloaded the gun. He took aim at the figures etched in the walls and sat the gun on his lap. The dull reflection of the fire held on the revolver. His coat lay folded once over on a flat rock. He brushed off the lapels and slipped the money into the inner pocket. He searched the front pockets and found the gift from Tobias. The single bead dangled off the pouch and below his hand. He untied the leather notch that held the contents firm. He pulled from it a dried root, both pungent and firm. The taste was of wet soil and dung. The canteen helped to loosen the pieces stuck to his teeth.

He sat along the wall of the cave, beyond the fingers of the dying fire. The circle of light that hovered in the center of the room rose, as if being pulled by an oozing gravity. Warmness took hold in his belly. His ears began to tune to a flapping in the room. It grew soft and raised low in front of him. He reached out to grab the noise. "Ye there!" Jack said. Palms outstretched toward the glow of the candles. The rabbit twitched, righted itself and hopped able-bodied out of the cave. His hand felt wet. "Rub ye hands on ye jeans," he said. Jack touched the light and stood over his jacket. He examined the small blood stain on the rock for which the rabbit lay. He ran his finger through the blood and he pressed down between the eyes of a buffalo and ran a red line down the snout of the beast. The blood did not run. The buffalo did not run. He stepped back and there the beast stood on a vast expanse. He placed his hand on the back of the animal. The short brown fur bunched in the lines of his palm. The beast steamed in the new light of the morning. The prairie stood dotted with moisture from a storm, shortly passed. The remnants of a wind shivered and swayed over the tops of the grass.

Awake. Jack peeled the side of his head from the coat he had folded and used as a pillow. The fire was cold, black and silent. The revolver lay under the jacket. He rubbed the side of his face. His cheek was stiff and sore from being pressed against the cylinder during the night. He checked the revolver and still loaded it was. The money untouched. A row of candles stood against the gallery wall. Short stubs sat lit and wax ran down the rock to the floor below. The cave was empty, with no clear sign of Shannon's return or the night's events. The rabbit was gone. The only trace a smear of blood. Jack thought of screaming but could not muster the word to yell. He rose slowly and noticed the scratch marks on his hands. Gathering his things, he approached the entrance to the cavern and saw the dim slither of light grow in clarity, as he inched through the narrow slabs.

8: HALF A MILE FROM TUCSON

Jack attempted to quietly step through the rocky passage. His footing shook under the uneven stones and sent echoes back down to the chamber. The passage was longer than he remembered and the light beaded in particles, as he inched toward the mouth of the cave. The light formed a white ball that pulsed in the rising heat of the desert morning. Jack put his foot on the rim of the cave and felt the thawing country crawl from the moon's grip. Over the crumbled and hacked piñon, a flycatcher darted between saguaro and the sun lay a soft haze over the valley. The cactus on the valley floor peeked from a long cloud lent from the sky. A voice said, "Fine morning." Jack jumped and there to his right, perched on a boulder above the cave, sat Shannon, with a grin as wide as the valley below. "Quite a sight. A real beauty. A real beauty," he said.

Jack took a deep breath and pointed at Shannon. "You damn fool. Ye nearly scared me into sending a scream down this valley. With half the territory ready to follow the alarm."

Shannon laughed and climbed down. "Not a soul out there, Jack. This valley here is empty of the human animal. Just about as long I been crouched here watching. Not a camp nor movement on the horizon for hours. Unless they jump round this mountain." Shannon looked up. Jack followed Shannon's eyes and looked up the massif, dressed in a green scrub that clung to its rocky flesh.

Shannon put his arm on Jack's shoulder. "You look ill. Yes. Your color is gone."

Jack said, "When did ye come back to the cave?"

"I didn't, Jack. You were there by your lonesome all night. By the time I ventured back, it was too dark to navigate the cave. My step was not what it was after the long ride yesterday and I had in mind what lies before us today. So, I curled up against the log there."

Jack looked over Shannon's shoulder. "And what lies before us today?"

"A trudge through this desert. Twenty-five mile or so I believe. I figure we do ten today, ten the next. We will be on board a train, pulling out of Tucson. Three days at the top."

"Three days? Horse should cover more than that."

Shannon drew his hands over his mouth. "Aye. The horse is gone."

"Gone? What ye mean?"

"I mean gone, Jack. No longer tied to the tree."

"What in the hell happened to it?"

"Don't right now. No blood. No tracks of the human kind."

"Damn. We're on foot in this desert?"

"We can make it, Jack."

Jack stepped around Shannon and looked down into the valley, toward the milky western horizon. "And you know the way?"

"I know what I was told by the old man. The poor fool has been on the dot so far. The plan was to travel west. Keeping the mountains to our right and on the second night, we should spot the lights of the city. From there, correct our bearings."

Jack squatted and ran his hand through the dirt. He raised his chin. "How much water is in that canteen?"

"If we keep to the ration and don't run our way into a spring? Two days."

"Two days." Jack coughed. "So, you slept out here?"

Knees buckled as they navigated down scree to the valley floor. The rocky slide offered the feeling that one was descending into a labyrinth of saguaro, where within a man could only expect to find barbed walls and madness. The sun baked the chiseled mountains as the men began to skirt the giants. Small arroyos of bear grass gave way to indigo and patches of ocotillo. The valley floor leveled and the walking was of little effort on the flat desert earth but the men scarcely spoke. The first break came sometime before noon. With little shade to speak of, they placed their backs to a mesquite of bare character and dipped their hats low. They took turns taking small but purposeful sips of the canteen. Jack dozed off in the sun; he awoke with Shannon shaking the top of his hat. "Wake up, Jack. Time to get the feet walking again. Come on, lad?"

Jack smacked his hand away. "Don't be shaking me awake. Man is liable to get himself shot that way. Even without trying."

The midday sun soon became a mass each man carried on his back. Under that solar weight, sweat was born from their pores and took the only course known in this world. Jack began to feel the bottoms of his feet slide in his wool socks and with it the sting of fresh sores. Each took turns bearing the small remnants of the dead man's possibles, but after moving on at noon, Jack threw the satchel into a patch of rotting maguey and moved on. The jerky was now at half ration each. The only eating after this share would be what could be killed and preferably eaten without fire. The sun stained the sky and ran the blue into white and faded behind the mountains. Shannon would mumble about keeping the formations to their right and they walked on. A cloud of dust on a far rise caught the attention of the travelers and they halted, watching it fade. "Was it riders?"

Shannon said, "I don't know."

A cold camp was broken for the night among a gathering of saguaro spears. The tallest of the bunch grew an arm pointing west. Shannon's hair was matted with red clay and he sat swaying in front of a rock. From his jacket pocket, Jack passed Shannon his remaining strip of the dead man's jerky. They tore and chewed in silence. Shannon looked up from studying the meal in his hands. "Tell me, Jack. How come you didn't shoot anything today?"

"I reckon I could have, if I'd seen a living creature in this damn desert. Getting the impression the only two fool enough to get on out here is us."

That night each man wrapped himself in his own arms and lay on the desert floor, with only coat as blanket and earth as pillow. The distant lights in the heavens looked down on them and in their eyes lay a map of countless galaxies that arched above them. Shannon said, "I will tell you one thing. After this, I will never fancy sleeping in the desert again. Only the finest living for me."

Morning came in a purple hue, one that warmed the dark hills, until clarity rang from the granite slopes and flickers made calls across the scrub. Walking on they came to a wash and followed the silt, twisted with sand and gravel, to the bottom. Traces of recent flow were drawn in the clay like footprints left in passing. A figure moved in the distance. Up on a rocky ledge, to the east, Shannon spotted the dead man's horse. They stopped. Jack raised his hand and shaded his brow. "What in all hell? Is that horse following us?" The horse lowered its ears and trotted off.

Shannon squatted and spat. "If you see the horse again. Shoot it."

The meridian of the sun found them tucked into the banks of the wash and they counted themselves lucky to find shade under the roots of an ironwood that hung from the rotting bank. There they cooled in the shadow of those crumbling roots. Each man with his eyes closed, not giving much care to be sprung upon by a posse, as only the devil would move in that heat. Eyes grew heavy and sweat stuck to the skin as if grease. The only detectable noise in that waste of high noon came from a cluster of creosote that hosted grasshoppers shaking their legs like a child's rattle. The cadence of such befitted an ancient rhythm, one that has gripped this land for millennia. Time passed and in that heat they became entranced with that rattle and none moved until the sun was full on to the other side of the wash and cut shade over the far bank. Jack rose first and lowered his hand toward Shannon. "Best get on," he said. Each slumped forth and after a short time, Shannon quickened their pace. "Next camp. The city should be in view." Jack shook his head and spat, dry and foamy.

They walked until a blue haze crept down on the land. The moon peeked over the mountains and the sun gave the satellite a ghostly orange hue as if a heavenly digit lay a smudge over the rocks of the thing. Jack nodded to Shannon and they both crouched upon the sight of a sizable rock squirrel, not more than twenty feet from their position. Jack drew the revolver and took a purposeful aim at the creature. The squirrel chewed on a seed and gazed off into that moon and that was indeed the creature's last heavenly view. Jack blew a hole through its spine. Shannon raised a yell and ran to fetch the carcass. Trotting back, Shannon held the hind of the creature toward the sky. Jack counted the three remaining bullets in the dead man's gun and tucked it back into the small of his back.

The debate over a fire was short, as the hunger bestowed on them from the long walk was final word on the matter. Agreed upon was a fire to roast and consume the meat but one not to linger over. The game was charred. Tough but neither complained. Jack sat picking his teeth with a small twig he whittled with the dead man's knife. Shannon sat across from the dying fire and watched him. He said, "Most likely you can see this fire for miles."

Jack looked over his shoulders. "From the right position."

Shannon rose. "I would offer up some coffee but we're closed. Let's move on."

Jack sucked on the twig. "'Bout now you can feel that noose round ye neck. Makes a man anxious."

Shannon kicked sand over the embers and off they set into a flat, clear night with the moon at their shoulder, giving the brush a radiance of azure. They moved through country thick with soap tree and overspread with dry rock flower. Down a bajada loose with basalt, they came to see headlands fading into the dusk. The distance was farther than assumed and the men were weak by the time they climbed a rockslide up into the pass. Their fingers ran the crevices carefully. Jack said, "If I get bit by a gila monster, ye sucking out the poison."

Shannon secured his footing atop a boulder and let out a laugh. "We'll just buy you the finest care in Tucson is all." Jack stood and Shannon pointed out toward small specks of shimmering light, bunched together on the black canvas of the valley floor. "Aye, Tomato Can. The old man told no tale. We climb down and find a spot to camp for the night. Tomorrow we make for the city at the crack. Come on." Shannon slid down the face of the stone and felt his way down the pass. Jack put his hands on his knees and gazed out on the sparse but sure light that outlined the capital of the territory.

Shannon led through silver-lined brush to a clearing and stopped at what appeared to be a fire ring in the moonlight. He put his hand over the surface of the charred wood. "Cold," he said. "Good a place as any."

Jack nodded. "How far we out of the city ye think?"

"Mile. Mile or two."

Jack slowly removed his left boot and peeled off his sock to inspect his blisters. "I reckon the same."

Around the fire ring they sat and stared into the black pit as if a fire danced within it. Jack rocked to ward off the cold and he soon decided his boots would not have time to air out tonight. The stiff leather made the pair difficult to slip back on. Jack said, "Might freeze to death out here tonight."

Shannon's arms were wrapped on the inside of his coat, and he matched Jack's motion. "If that is the case, they will find two rich, stiff corpses."

Mockingbirds called in the night. The moon was pinned to a curtain of stars that draped over the country. Shannon rubbed his eyes and found Jack staring at him from across the naked firepit. Jack coughed and shook his head. "This cold air. Gets on my throat. Sitting here like this bringin' back some old memories. It does. It does. We broke a cold camp on the trail often. I'd taken up with an outfit traveling down the Chisholm, to pick up on work coming up the trail. I was about as green as they came in them days. They figured me working the wagon. And that's what I was fixing to do when I got my shot. Anyhow, we came to settle down for the night in Caldwell. The crew there had been spooked by some hostiles so. No fire, they says. No fire. They was out there ready to take our eyes out and skew them in the fire. And that's what one of them cowboys told me. Reckon they was correct. So we sat there eating cold day-old beans. We all sat just like this. Staring into an unlit fire. Wrapped in wool blankets. Instead of these weeds around us. There was cattle. Looked like a million head to me back then. There we sat. On the end of this slumbering herd, ready to be sprung on by Indians."

Jack coughed again. "Damn. The moon was high. Not a man spoke among us. Now, must have been well late when this figure comes riding into camp. Half of the cowboys was sure it was the start of a war and the other half just sat waiting for their heads to be split open. I won't mention which one I was. This rider comes in under the watch of about six rifles and if the boy was not the luckiest son of a bitch you ever met. Just about when he was going to lose his head, he calls out, 'I'm white. Throw down ye arms!' Well just about everyone fell down laughing."

"The fella comes on in. Comes down off his horse and says, 'Boy named Straw here? Jack Straw from Wichita?' I didn't know what to think about it. I stood. 'That's me, mister,' I said. He parts the cowboys and comes straight up to me and says, 'Son, I am afraid I have bad news for ye. Your mother passed.' I just stood frozen on that ground and all I could hear was the cattle moving about. Chewing and fidgeting and hooves stamping down on the matted grass. I can't remember much of the rest of the night. One of the cowboys handed me a bottle of whiskey. Ended up passing out. The next morning came to, 'bout noon time. Out cold I was. I rubbed my eyes and the cattle was gone. Just some of the boys waiting on me to stir. The rider was gone. He made back for Wichita. My uncle paid the man five dollars to catch up to me and give me the news. There was no other instruction or any other part to the message. Just she had passed. The man rode fifty-some miles to tell me and rode on back. Suppose he needed the money."

Jack looked toward the pass. A coyote howled over their camp. Shannon rubbed the back of his neck. "And then what?" he said.

"Then what? The boys said I need to make a choice. Go on back to Wichita or continue down the trail. Wasn't much of a choice then. Can't say I know what I likely would choose now. I rode on. Not far though. Made it only to Red River. Trail was all but dried up. I found work going as far as Abilene. But not in the cards, as a man of your persuasion might say. In Ryan, I caught a fever and the crew left me where they carried me off the wagon. I was alone. Broke. Had me a horse though. Pointed her south. That direction led me right here. Over a cold fire in the desert. Across from you."

The coyote howled once more. Shannon shifted his eyes. "Closer," he said. "With no fire something will come sniff us out."

"Maybe even that damn horse."

Shannon rose and stepped toward the moon and gazed into the face of the rock that illuminated the mountains below in clear silver shadow. "And what of this spot you sit now, Jack? This direction? Where will you point the horse next, lad?" Jack studied Shannon. Shannon turned and the moon crowned a halo over his head. He stood staring down at Jack. Shannon said, "Best get some sleep. Early rise tomorrow."

Jack looked up at the blackness between the constellations and said, "I dream of beasts now. I dream of beasts." Shannon lay down on the desert floor and both men slept sound.

The sun laid a blanket over the country that morning, the saguaro-like islands poking up from the comfort of the embrace. Shannon was up with the earliest suggestion of the day. He shook Jack's leg. "Aye, go time. Go time." They set off slowly, stepping through thick bear grass and patches of graythorn. After an hour of walking, Shannon said, "Longer than a mile." The city shimmered in the fledgling heat, as if a mirage just out of reach.

Jack scratched his ear hard. "Damn all. Think something got me last night."

Shannon stopped to listen but then moved on. "Come on, Jack. Just a mile to go."

Jack fell back. He removed his jacket, tossing the dusty garment over his shoulder. His pace was half that of Shannon, who would stop and look back at his partner and shake his head. The sun had replaced the moon. A dip in the terrain. Shannon was out of view to Jack and Jack to him. When Jack came down off the rise, there sat Shannon on a rock with hat in hand. He shrugged his shoulders. "You're moving much too slow today, Jack. Much too slow."

Jack approached and rested his right foot upon rock. "How far ye reckon?"

Shannon looked out at Tucson. He squinted. "Clear as day, isn't she? Half mile, I presume. Hard to tell in this desert. Can you keep up?"

Jack looked out at the city and said, "Yes."

Shannon rubbed his eye with the knuckle of his thumb. "Damn sand. Come on then." Shannon rose.

Jack called to him and when Shannon turned, Jack steadied the dead man's revolver and fired a single round into Shannon's chest. The shot bounced off the foothills and the mist the sun brought down on the land dissipated. Clarity rang over that country and Jack looked about and saw the beauty and wonder. He searched the ground for some time before finding a flat hunk of ironwood that would serve well as a shovel. Next to a coursetia, he dug a shallow grave. He was shirtless by the time he had finished. He stripped Shannon down to his underwear and there he lay his body down. He covered his body with earth and scrub and large stones. Stripping the area of all he could, Jack emptied the remaining two bullets and broke the dead man's revolver against a rock. After scattering the pieces in a thicket of bear grass, he returned and crouched over the grave. He removed his hat. Jack looked off toward the sun and the scarred mountains. A wind came down the valley and the coursetia shook. A lek of butterflies scattered off a desert bloom. Jack rose and patted his back pockets to ensure the folded bills were on his person. He turned toward Tucson and walked on.